the

SPAGHETTI DETECTIVES

the

SPAGHETTI DETECTIVES

Andreas Steinhöfel

translated from the German
by Chantal Wright

Chicken House

SCHOLASTIC INC. / NEW YORK

First published in Germany as *Rico, Oskar und die Tieferschatten* by Carlsen Verlag GmbH, Hamburg.
Original text copyright © 2008 by Carlsen Verlag GmbH, Hamburg
English translation copyright © 2010 by Chantal Wright

First published in English in the United Kingdom in 2010 as *The Pasta Detectives* by Chicken House, 2 Palmer Street, Frome, Somerset BA11 1DS.
www.doublecluck.com

Library of Congress Cataloging-in-Publication Data

Steinhöfel, Andreas.

[Rico, Oskar und die Tieferschatten. English]
The spaghetti detectives / by Andreas Steinhöfel ; [translation by Chantal Wright].
—1st American ed.

    p. cm.

Summary: Living with his mother in a Berlin apartment house, Rico, a young boy with ADHD, enjoys playing detective games, but when his friend Oscar suddenly disappears, possibly taken by a serial kidnapper, Rico determines to use his skills to find his friend.

ISBN 978-0-545-28975-7

[1. Mystery and detective stories. 2. Attention-deficit hyperactivity disorder—Fiction. 3. Single-parent families—Fiction. 4. Apartment houses—Fiction. 5. Friendship—Fiction. 6. Berlin (Germany)—Fiction. 7. Germany—Fiction.] I. Wright, Chantal. II. Title.

PZ7.S82635Sp 2011

10 9 8 7 6 5 4 3 2 1   11 12 13 14 15

Printed in the U.S.A.   23
First American edition, July 2011

The text type was set in Amasis.
The display type was set in TF2 Secondary Type and Geometric Slabserif.
Book design by Elizabeth B. Parisi and Whitney Lyle

For Gianni . . .
from me to you
and back again
—A.S.

SATURDAY
spaghetti surprise

The string of spaghetti lay on the sidewalk. It was thin and tacky and twelve inches long. Some dried-up cheese sauce and dirt were stuck to it. I picked it up, cleaned off the dirt, and looked up past the old windows of 93 Dieffe Street into the summer sky. Not a cloud in sight, and definitely none of those white stripes that jet engines leave behind. And besides, I thought, I don't think you can just open an airplane window and throw out your food.

I let myself into my apartment building, whizzed up the yellow-painted stairway to the third floor, and rang Mrs. Darling's bell. She had large, bright curlers in her hair, just as she did every Saturday.

"Could be capellini. The sauce is definitely Gorgonzola," she declared. "It's nice of you to bring me the string of spaghetti, dear, but *I* didn't throw it out the window. Why don't you ask Mr. Fitz?"

She grinned at me, tapped one finger against her forehead, rolled her eyes, and looked up at the ceiling. Mr. Fitz lives on the fourth floor. I hate him. Also I don't think the string of spaghetti is his. Mrs. Darling was my first choice, because she often throws things out the window. Last winter she threw out a television. Followed five minutes later by her husband, but he came out the front door. After that she came down to see us, and Mom had to pour her a drop of whiskey.

"He has a girlfriend!" Mrs. Darling had exclaimed in shock. "And she's not even younger than I am! Give me another swig of that stuff!"

The very next day, with the television in smithereens and her husband gone, she bought herself an amazing new flat-screen TV and DVD player. We sometimes watch romantic comedies or thrillers together, but only on the weekend when Mrs. Darling can have a lazy day. During the week she works behind the butcher's counter at a supermarket. Her hands are always red-raw because it's so cold in there.

When we watch television we eat whole wheat crackers with boiled ham and eggs or canned sardines. If it's a romantic comedy, Mrs. Darling sniffs her way through at least ten tissues, then starts complaining about the movie: "As if that sort of thing really happens! When a man and a woman get together is when the misery begins, but of course they never show *that* in the movies. What a pack of lies! Another cracker, Rico?"

"Are we still on for this evening?" Mrs. Darling called after me as I ran up to the fourth floor, two steps at a time.

"Course!"

Her door banged shut and I knocked at Mr. Fitz's. You always have to knock at Mr. Fitz's. His bell is broken. In fact it probably has been since they built the apartments in 1910.

I had to wait, wait, wait.

And listen to the *shuffle, shuffle, shuffle* behind the old, wooden door.

Finally Mr. Fitz appeared, dressed, as usual, in his dark blue pajamas with the gray stripes. His wrinkled face was covered in stubble and his stringy gray hair shot up from his head in all directions.

What a mess!

A strong smell of mold wafted out. Who knew what Mr. Fitz kept in there? In his apartment, I mean, not in his head. I tried to look past him without him noticing, but he stood in my way. Deliberately! I've been in every apartment in the building except his. Mr. Fitz won't let me in because he doesn't like me.

"Ah, the little dimwit," he growled.

At this point I should explain that my name is Rico and that I am a child proddity. That's a bit like being a child prodigy, but also like the opposite. I think an awful lot, but I need a lot of time to figure things out. (Some people find this odd.) There's nothing wrong with my brain, though. It's a perfectly normal size. Only sometimes a few things go missing, and unfortunately I never know when or where it's going to happen. And I can't always concentrate very well when I'm telling a story. I have a mind like a sieve — at least I think it's a sieve, it could be a cheese grater or a whisk . . . and now you see my problem.

My head is sometimes as topsy-turvy as a barrel full of lottery balls. I play bingo every Tuesday with Mom at the Gray Bumblebees senior citizens' club and they have a drum full of bingo balls there, which is just the same. I have no idea why Mom enjoys going there so much, because it really is only for retirees. Some of them never seem to go home, because they wear the same clothes every week — just like Mr. Fitz and his one pair of pajamas — and a few of them smell kind of funny. Maybe Mom likes it so much because she wins all the time. She beams every time she goes onstage to collect one of those cheap plastic handbags — she only ever wins cheap plastic handbags, in fact.

The senior citizens don't really notice. A lot of them fall asleep over their bingo cards or don't follow what's going on. Just a few weeks ago one of them sat completely still at a table the whole time the numbers were being called. When the others left, he didn't get up, and when the cleaning lady finally tried to wake him up, she realized he was dead. Mom thought he might already have been dead the Tuesday before. I thought so, too.

"Hello, Mr. Fitz," I said, "I hope I didn't wake you up."

Mr. Fitz looks even older than the retiree who dropped dead at bingo. And he's really stinky dirty. Apparently he doesn't have long to live, either. That's why he wears his pajamas all the time, even when he goes to the supermarket. When he does drop dead, at least he'll be wearing the right clothes. Mr. Fitz once told Mrs. Darling he's had a heart problem ever since he was very small. That's why he gets out of breath so easily, he said, and one day it'll be *KA-POW!* But even if he is about to die, he could still get dressed, or at least wash his pajamas sometimes. At Christmas, for example. I wouldn't like to collapse in front of the cheese counter at the supermarket and smell totally gross, not when I'd only just died that minute.

Mr. Fitz stared at me, so I thrust the string of spaghetti under his nose. "Is this yours?"

"Where did you get that?"

"The sidewalk. Mrs. Darling thinks it could be capellini. The sauce is definitely Gorgonzola."

"Was it just lying there?" he asked suspiciously. "Or was it lying in something?"

"Huh?"

"Where's your brain gone? The string of spaghetti, you dimwit!"

"What was the question again?"

Mr. Fitz rolled his eyes. Any minute now he would explode.

"For goodness' sake! Was your string of spaghetti just lying there on the sidewalk, or was it lying in something? Dog poo, for instance."

"It was just lying there," I said.

"Then let me take a closer look."

He took the string of spaghetti and turned it around in his fingers. Then he put it—my string of spaghetti!—into his mouth and swallowed it. Without chewing.

And then he slammed the door. *KER-ASH!*

He's not right in the head!! The next string of spaghetti I find, I'm going to drop it in dog poo, wiggle it around a bit, then bring it to Mr. Fitz, and when he asks if it was lying in something, I'm going to tell him it's meat sauce.

I had really wanted to ask everybody who lived in the building about that string of spaghetti, but now it was gone, swallowed up by Mr. Fitz. I was sad. It's always like that when you lose something. When I had it I didn't think it was that great, but now it was suddenly the best string of spaghetti in the world. That was how it was with Mrs. Darling. Last winter she was moaning about her husband being a cheat, and now she's watching one romantic comedy after another and wishing he'd come back.

I wanted to go down to the second floor, but I thought it over and rang the doorbell of the apartment opposite Mr. Fitz's first. That was where the new person who moved in two days before lived. I hadn't seen him yet. I didn't have the string of spaghetti anymore, but it seemed like a good time to say hello. Maybe he'd let me in. I like visiting other people's apartments.

This apartment had been empty for a long time because it was so expensive. Mom had thought about renting it. There's more light on the fourth floor than on the second and even a bit of a view. You can look out through the trees over the old, flat-roofed hospital on the other side of the road. But when Mom found out what the apartment would cost, she had to drop the idea. Luckily for me, because then Mr. Fitz would have been right next door to us.

The new person's name was Mr. Westhaven. That's what it said on the sign under the doorbell. He wasn't at home, and I was actually a little bit happy about that. It made me nervous, thinking that I'd have to say his name out loud. East and west, if you see what I mean. I always get left and right mixed up, even on the compass. When it's a matter of left or right, the lottery balls in my head always start to jumble.

I was angry as I ran down the stairs. If Mr. Fitz hadn't destroyed my evidence, it would have been a great day to be a detective. The pool of suspects was very small. For example, I could rule out the two fancy apartments on the fifth floor. The Kaminsky-Kowalskys had gone on vacation the day before, and Mr. Marrak, who lives next door to them, hadn't been seen for two whole days. He was probably staying at his girlfriend's, who also did his laundry for him. Every few weeks Mr. Marrak could be seen running around with a giant bag of laundry. He ran out of the building, back into the building, back out, back in, and on and on it went. Mrs. Darling once said that the young men of today were useless. Once upon a time they would just take a toothbrush with them when they went out, and today they took half their wardrobe. Mr. Marrak wasn't at home, in any case. Yesterday's junk mail was still sticking out of his mailbox in the hall downstairs. If you watch murder mysteries instead of smoochy movies, you start noticing things like that right away.

OK, that was the fifth floor crossed off. Mr. Fitz and the new man with the compass thing in his name live on the fourth floor. On the third floor, across from Mrs. Darling, lives Mr. Kirk. There's no point knocking on his door until the evening, anyway, because he's out at work during the day. He works as a dental technician in a laboratory.

On the floor below are Mom and me, and across from us the six Kesslers, two adults and four children, but they're on vacation, too. The Kesslers own their apartment and there's a staircase connecting their second-floor apartment with their other apartment on the floor below. Mr. and Mrs. Kessler need a lot of space with all those kids.

Most of all I had been looking forward to visiting the other apartment on the first floor, the one below Mom and me. That's where Julie lives, along with Bert and Massoud. They're students. But I couldn't go and knock without the string of spaghetti. Bert is all right. I can't stand Massoud, because Julie likes him more than me. And that's all I'm saying on that subject for the moment. I should have started my investigation down there, or at old Mr. Mommsen's, the superintendent—he lives on the ground floor.

Oh well, never mind.

So it's back to the second floor, and home.

As I went into the apartment, Mom was standing in the

hall in front of the gold mirror with the little fat cherubs on it. She was looking at herself in a worried way and prodding her body all over. I could see her thoughtful face in the mirror.

A lot of people stare at Mom in the street. She looks fantastic. She always wears short skirts and low-cut tops. High-heeled, silver or gold strappy sandals. Her blonde hair loose, long, and silky, and a whole bunch of ringing, jingling bracelets, chains, and earrings. I like her fingernails best of all. They're really long. Mom glues something new onto them every week. Tiny glittering fish, or a small ladybug on each one, for example.

"At some point everything's going to start sagging," Mom said to her reflection in the mirror and to me. "Another two or three years and gravity will have its way. Life's all about crossing off the days."

I didn't know what gravity was. I would have to look it up. I always look up things I don't know in the dictionary, so that I get smarter. Or sometimes I ask people. Mom or Mrs. Darling or my teacher, Mr. Meyer. I write down what I've discovered. Like this:

GRAVITY: When something is heavier than something else, it pulls the other thing toward it. For example, the earth is heavier than almost everything else, that's why nothing falls off it. A man called Isaac Newton discovered gravity. It is dangerous for apples. And possibly for other round things, too.

"What will you do then?" I said.

"Then I'll have a tune-up," Mom said decisively. She sighed and turned to me. "How was school?"

"All right."

She knows not to say anything about my special classes, because I hate talking about them. For years Mr. Meyer has been trying to sort out the lottery balls in my head. I've thought about suggesting that he should turn off the lottery machine before he starts messing around with the balls, but I never actually have. If he doesn't know that, that's his tough luck.

"Why did Mr. Meyer ask you to come in today?" said Mom. "I thought yesterday was the last day of school."

"It was for a summer project. Some writing."

"You, writing?" She wrinkled up her forehead. "What are you writing?"

"Just something about me," I murmured. It was more complicated than that, but I didn't want to let Mom in on it until I'd tried it out successfully.

"I see." Her forehead smoothed out. "Have you had anything to eat?" She ran one hand through my hair, leaned over, and kissed me on the forehead.

"Nah."

"So you're hungry?"

"Yeah."

"OK. I'll make us some fish sticks." She disappeared into the kitchen. I tossed my backpack through the open door into my bedroom, then followed her, sat at the dinner table, and watched.

"I need to ask you something, Rico," Mom said as she melted butter in the pan—fried in butter is how we like fish sticks best.

My head automatically slipped down between my shoulders. Whenever Mom asks me something and uses my name at the same time, that means she's been thinking about things, and when she's been thinking about things, it's usually something serious. And by serious I mean difficult. And by difficult I mean lottery balls.

"What?" I asked cautiously.

"It's about Mr. 2000."

I wished the fish sticks were already done. Even an idiot could tell where this conversation was going.

Mom opened the fridge, scraping and digging around in the freezer compartment with a knife to free the packet of fish sticks from its covering of blue ice. "He let another child go," she continued. "That's the fifth already."

Mr. 2000 has been keeping everybody in Berlin on the edge of their seats for three months. On television they said he was probably the most cunning child kidnapper of all time. Some people call him the ALDI kidnapper, after the cut-price supermarket, because his ransoms are so low. He lures little boys and girls into his car and drives off with them, and afterward he writes their parents a letter:

DEAR PARENTS: IF YOU WOULD LIKE LITTLE CLAUDIA BACK, IT WILL COST YOU ONLY 2000 EUROS. THINK CAREFULLY BEFORE GETTING THE POLICE INVOLVED OVER SUCH A RIDICULOUSLY SMALL SUM, BECAUSE IF YOU DO, YOUR CHILD WILL COME BACK TO YOU PIECE BY PIECE.

Up until now none of the parents have told the police until after they had paid up and their child popped up safe. But everybody in Berlin is waiting for the day when some little Claudia or Alexander doesn't come home in one piece because their parents have messed up. Maybe some people would be secretly happy that their child had been kidnapped and wouldn't cough up a penny. Or they might be really poor and only have fifty euros to their name. If you only gave Mr. 2000 fifty euros, it's likely that the only piece left of your child would be a hand. The interesting question is what would he send back—the hand or the rest of the body? My bets are on the hand. It would be less noticeable. And a giant box for everything-minus-the-hand would cost fifty euros in postage all by itself.

If you ask me, two thousand euros is a ton of money. But in an emergency, as Bert once explained to me, anybody can get their hands on the cash if they put their mind to it. Bert is studying for an Em-Bee-Ay, which has something to do with money, so he must know what he's talking about.

"Do you have two thousand euros?" I asked Mom. You need to be prepared. In an emergency she could break into my piggy bank. I've had it for as long as I can remember and I'm pretty sure I must have saved enough for an arm or a leg. For twenty or thirty euros, Mom would at least have a small piece to remember me by.

"Two thousand euros," she said. "Who do you think I am?"

"Would you be able to get that much money?"

"For you? Even if I had to kill for it, love."

There was a crack and a thick piece of ice landed on the kitchen floor. Mom picked it up, made a noise like *pfff* or *hhmmph*, and threw it into the sink. "This freezer really needs defrosting."

"But I'm not as small as the kids who were kidnapped. And I'm older."

"Yeah, I know." She pried the packet open. "But I should still have taken you to school every day for the last few weeks, and picked you up again."

Mom works until early in the morning. When she comes home, she brings me a fresh bread roll and gives me a kiss before I leave for school, and then she goes to bed. She usually doesn't get up until the afternoon, long after I'm back home again. She would never manage to take me to school and pick me up again.

She held her breath for a second and scratched her nose. "Am I a bad mother, Rico?"

"Of course not!"

She looked at me thoughtfully for a moment, then tipped the deep-frozen fish sticks out of the packet and into the pan.

The butter was so hot that it hissed. Mom took a quick step back. "Oh God! Now I stink of the stuff!"

She would shower anyway before going to work that night. She always showers after fish sticks. It's the most expensive perfume in the world, she once said; nothing sticks to you like the smell of fish sticks, and that's the real reason they're called sticks, she said. So you have to wash lots. While they were sizzling in the pan, I told her about the string of spaghetti I'd found and that Mr. Fitz had destroyed it, which was why I couldn't find out who it had belonged to.

"The old grouch," she murmured.

Mom can't stand Mr. Fitz. A few years ago, when we moved into 93 Dieffe Street, she dragged me through the entire building so that we could introduce ourselves to the neighbors. Her hand was very sweaty, and she held me really tightly. Mom is brave, but she still has feelings. She was afraid that people wouldn't like us when they found out she worked in a nightclub and I was a bit different. Mr. Fitz answered her knock and stood there in his pajamas. Unlike Mom, who kept a straight face, I grinned. That was my mistake. And then Mom said, "Hello, I've just moved in, and this is my son, Rico. He's a bit different, but it's not his fault. So if he ever bothers you . . ."

Mr. Fitz squinted at us and made a face as though he had a bad taste in his mouth. Then, without saying a word, he slammed the door in our faces. Ever since then he's called me a dimwit.

"Did he call you a dimwit?" Mom asked.

"Nah." There was no point getting her worked up.

"The old grouch," she said again.

She didn't ask why I absolutely had to know who the string of spaghetti belonged to. That was just another one of Rico's ideas, and she was right. There was no point asking.

I watched her as she turned the fish sticks. She hummed a song and shifted her weight from the left foot to the right and back again. While the fish sticks were frying, she set the table. The sun fell through the window and there was the tasty smell of summer and fish in the air. I felt happy. I like it when Mom cooks or does one of those other look-aftering things that moms do.

"Blood sauce?" she said when she was finished.

"Yep."

She put the bottle of ketchup on the table and pushed my plate toward me. "So I won't be taking you to school, then?"

I shook my head. "It's summer vacation now, anyway. Maybe they'll catch him before school starts."

"Are you sure?"

"Yeeesss!"

"Good."

She was shoveling down the fish sticks at top speed. "I have to go in a sec," she said in reply to my questioning look. "I'm going to the hairdresser's with Irina." Irina is Mom's best friend. She works at the club, too. "Strawberry blonde—what do you think?"

"Is that red?"

"No. It's blonde with a hint of red."

"What's that got to do with strawberries?"

"They have a hint of it, too."

"Strawberries are bright red."

"Only when they're ripe."

"But before that they're green. And what sort of hint is it?"

"That's just what they call it."

Mom doesn't like it when I keep on at her, and I don't like it when she talks and I don't understand what she's saying. Some things have really silly names, and you have to ask why they're called what they're called. I wonder, for example, why strawberries are called strawberries, even though they've got nothing to do with straw.

Mom pushed away her empty plate. "We still need a few things for the weekend. I could pick up the stuff myself, but . . ."

"I'll do it."

"You're a love." She grinned with relief, got up, and hurriedly rummaged through her pockets. "I made a list, hang on a sec . . ."

Mom's jeans are so tight I'm afraid I'll have to cut her out of them one of these days. I ask myself why she always stuffs everything into her jeans pockets. She's won at least ten plastic handbags at bingo, but she never uses them. She doesn't even keep them. She auctions them off on eBay.

"It's not much." She held out the crumpled shopping list. "There's money in the drawer. The most important thing is the toothpaste. And butter's not on the list, but there's none left. Will you remember, or should I . . . ?"

I speared the first fish stick with my fork and casually dunked it in the blood sauce. "I'll remember," I said.

Hopefully.

SATURDAY AGAIN
oscar

The shopping went really well. Toothpaste, butter, bread sticks, salad stuff, and yogurt. I held out the money to the woman at the cash register and she gave me my change and said to say hello to my mom. The way she said it, she looked as though she actually wished Mom a really painful death. After we moved to Dieffe Street, Mom went in to see her to explain politely that I can't do arithmetic and that the last person who tried to cheat me had lived to regret it.

I went out of the shop. There was a light wind moving the leaves on the trees in the street—I've forgotten what they're called, or I never knew, but they look great. The bark on their trunks peels off like varnish on an old door and underneath you can see lighter bark that's also peeling off, and more underneath that. You have to ask yourself if it does that all the way through.

Sunlight shone down on millions of leaves and threw tiny shadows onto the sidewalk. There were people everywhere, lots of them sitting outside in front of coffee shops and restaurants, and music from the open windows of the apartments made its way down to the street. I was very happy at that moment. I felt good about myself.

Dieffe Street is very long and has everything you need. The supermarket and a late-night corner shop, two fruit and vegetable shops, a liquor store, a baker, butcher—those kinds of places. You don't have to turn off anywhere, and that's why Mom picked such a long, straight street for me to live on: because I don't remember the way very well if it has corners. Mom says my sense of direction is like a drunken pigeon in a windy snowstorm. But from Dieffe Street I can actually go to school by myself. All I have to do is go out of the house, walk a little way to the drugstore on the corner and then turn off upward, in the direction of the canal. From then on I keep going straight, across the bridge to school. The street keeps going past the school, through Little Istanbul toward the subway station, but I've never been brave enough to go any farther than the kebab restaurant, just *before* the station.

I wondered if I should look for another string of spaghetti on the way home. Maybe it hadn't flown out the window at 93 Dieffe Street, but a passerby had lost it or dropped it on purpose instead.

PASSERBY: Pedestrian. Had to ask Mom what we call them again. It's bad enough translating foreign words into words you understand. The other way around is even harder.

I shuffled along and thought about Hansel and Gretel, who laid a trail of bread crumbs in the forest so they wouldn't get lost. Maybe somebody in the area laid a trail of spaghetti strings. If they did, then they are even more of a child proddity than I am. They'll never find their way back when there are greedy pigs like Mr. Fitz around. Hansel and Gretel had their trail of crumbs eaten up by the birds of the forest, and where did the two of them end up? That's right, with the big bad wolf!

I stopped at the playground. The playground is framed by Grimm Street; it loops around up by the canal and comes back down to meet Dieffe Street, so it's kind of a double street. The playground is large and always full of moms and toddlers when the weather is good. In the part of the city where we lived before we moved here, Mom often went to the playground with me. I had a shovel and a sieve and all kinds of sand buckets to play with, until I dug a hole and threw them in it. I covered them all up with my hands and never found any of them again.

I looked at the playground a little longer and smiled at the little kids for a bit, then I remembered the string of spaghetti. I walked slowly over the pavement, looking at the gray cobblestones. I saw a scrunched-up chocolate wrapper, a few pieces of glass lying on the ground in front of the big recycling containers, and an old cigarette butt. Then I saw small feet wearing brightly colored socks in sandals.

I raised my head. The boy who was standing there in front of me only came up as far as my chest. That is to say, his dark blue crash helmet only came up as far as my chest. It was the kind of crash helmet that motorcycle riders wear. I didn't know you could get them in children's sizes, too. He looked like he had a screw loose. The see-through thing on his helmet was pushed up.

VISOR: A see-through thing. I asked Bert about it because he rides a motorcycle. He told me that Julie and Massoud had gone on vacation together. Hmph . . .

"What are you doing?" the boy said. His teeth were enormous. They looked as though they could tear entire pieces out of large animals: horses or giraffes or animals like that.

"I'm looking for something."

"If you tell me what it is, I can help you."

"A piece of pasta."

He searched the pavement. As he lowered his head, a beam of sunlight struck his helmet and bounced off it. I noticed a tiny, bright red toy airplane fastened to his short-sleeved shirt with a safety pin, like a badge. One of the airplane's wings had broken off. The small boy also looked in the bushes in front of the playground fence; I hadn't thought of that.

"What kind of pasta is it?" he said.

"Definitely a lost piece. Capellini, but I'm not sure. I won't know that until I find it, otherwise it wouldn't be lost."

"Hmm . . ." He put his head to one side. The mouth with the large teeth opened wide. "Are you not all there, brains-wise?"

Well, thanks a lot!

"I'm a child proddity."

"Is that a fact?" Now he looked really interested. "I'm a child prodigy."

Now I was interested, too. Even though the boy was much smaller than I was, he suddenly felt much bigger. It was a strange feeling. We looked at each other for such a long time that I thought we would still be standing there when the sun went down. I had never seen a child prodigy, apart from on TV in one of those talent contests. There was a girl who played something really difficult on the violin and at the same time the host of the show called out numbers a mile long and she had to say if they were prime numbers or not. Mrs. Darling swallowed down a Mallomar in one go and said that the little girl would go far in life, which is why I thought prime numbers were something important. Turns out they're not.

PRIME NUMBER: A prime number is a number that you can only divide by the number 1 and by itself, if you want to avoid fractures. Broken arms, for example. If I had been that TV host, I would have asked the girl why she didn't play the flute or the trumpet instead of the violin. That way, if you fracture your arm, you can keep on blowing.

"I've got to go now," I said to the boy finally. "Before it gets dark. Otherwise I might get lost."

"Where do you live?"

"Over there, in the yellow building. Number 93. On the right."

I could have kicked myself as soon as I said *on the right*. First of all I didn't really know if it was on the right—it might have been on the left. Secondly the old hospital is across from the row of apartment buildings, stretched out like a sleeping cat, and you can tell right away that that isn't a building where people live.

The boy followed my outstretched arm. When he saw number 93, he wrinkled up his forehead as though he had just made an amazing discovery and then wrinkled it down again as though he was thinking deeply about something.

Finally his forehead smoothed out and he grinned. "You're really not all there, are you? If something is right in front of you and all you've got to do is keep going straight, you can't possibly get lost."

At least I'd got the right side of the street. I was getting just a little angry, anyway. "Oh yeah? Well, *I* can. And if you are really as smart as you say you are, you would know that there are people who can."

"I—"

"And another thing. It's not funny at all!"

All the lottery balls had turned red and were clacking against each other. "It's not my fault that sometimes things go missing from my brain! I don't mean to be stupid. I'm not stupid because I'm lazy!"

"Hey, I—"

"I bet you're one of those superbrains who knows everything and always has to show off about something because otherwise nobody is interested in them unless they play the violin on TV!"

It's very embarrassing, but when I get really worked up about something, when something isn't fair, for example, I start to cry. There's absolutely nothing I can do about it. The boy looked shocked under his crash helmet.

"Don't cry! I didn't mean to—"

"And I know what a prime number is!" I shouted.

I was upset, that was about the only thing I did know at that moment. The boy didn't say anything else. He looked down at his sandals. Then he looked up again. He stretched out his hand. It was so small that both of his would have fit into one of mine.

"I'm Oscar," he said. "And I would like to apologize sincerely. I shouldn't have made fun of you. It was arrogant."

I had no idea what he meant by the last word, but I understood he was sorry.

ARROGANT: When somebody looks down on somebody else. So Oscar can't be all that smart because at the end of the day he's a lot smaller than I am and has to keep looking up at me.

You have to be nice when somebody apologizes. If somebody is just pretending, you can keep on being mad, but Oscar meant it sincerely. He'd said so himself.

"I'm Rico," I said, and shook his hand. "My dad was Italian."

"Is he dead?"

"Of course. Otherwise I wouldn't have said *was*." My teacher, Mr. Meyer, told me that one of the strengths of my writing is the tenses: the past, present, and future, and the if-I-were-you tense.

"I'm sorry. How did he die?"

I didn't answer. I've never told anybody how my dad died. It's nobody's business. It's a very sad story. I wrinkled my nose, looked over the fence at the playground, and tried to think of something else. For example, whether there were shovels and buckets and sieves buried there, too, and if so, how many and which colors. There were probably hundreds. If I dug them up, Mom could auction them off on eBay with her handbags.

Oscar wasn't sure what to do when he realized I wasn't going to say anything else. At some point he nodded his head and said, "I have to go home now."

"Me too. Otherwise the butter will melt." I lifted up the shopping bag. And then, because he looked so neat and tidy in his funny clothes, like one of those kids who have to eat fruit and vegetables and sugar-free muesli from the health food shop, I said, "We ran out of butter because we had fish sticks with blood sauce for lunch today."

I walked off and decided not to turn around. I didn't want to give him the impression that I thought he was great with his crash helmet and his monster teeth. But then I did turn around after all and I saw him disappearing down Dieffe Street in the other direction. From a distance he looked like a very small child with a very large blue head.

It was only when I was back at home and I'd put the butter in the fridge and begun to scrape the ice out of the freezer compartment that I realized I hadn't asked Oscar what he was doing there all by himself on our block. Or why he had a small, bright red airplane on his shirt. Or why he was wearing a motorcycle crash helmet, even though he was on foot.

Mrs. Darling's curls had turned out very nicely. I gave her the bread sticks as she let me in. The evening light was all red-golden and fell into the hallway through the open door of the living room. There were little pictures in plastic frames all over the walls; most of them contained drawings of small children with very large eyes who were standing in different places—in front of the Eiffel Tower, or on a bridge in Venice, for example. There were pictures with clowns, too, and other things. Half of the children were crying.

"I'm not doing too well, my dear," said Mrs. Darling, and closed the door to the apartment. "I'm having one of my gray days."

I almost cheered. A gray day meant that we wouldn't be

watching a romantic film. I've got nothing against them, but they make me a little bit nervous. There are no romantic films about proddities — it's as though nobody loves people like me. OK, there's *Forrest Gump*, but that film doesn't have a happy ending, and I can't stand Forrest, anyway. He's so pushy and greedy.

Mrs. Darling placed a hand on my shoulder and guided me into her living room. I'm not so stupid that I would lose my way in her little apartment, but I didn't say anything. Her gray days aren't easy and you have to be a bit nice to her.

"Did you find out who the string of spaghetti belonged to? Was it Mr. Fitz?"

"Nah."

I didn't tell her that the stupid man had swallowed it up. I planted myself on the sofa and glanced at the table. There was a plate on it full of boiled ham, pickled onions, and tomato halves. My stomach started rumbling.

"If it wasn't Mr. Fitz," she thought out loud, "then it was probably one of those Kessler brats."

"Nah. The Kesslers are on vacation. They went yesterday. Just like the Kaminsky-Kowalskys."

The Kesslers have been on TV and in the paper and everything. They're a sensation because Mrs. Kessler had two sets of twins in the same year: two boys in January, two girls in December. They just about manage to fit in Christmas and New Year's between the two sets of birthdays. Expensive piece of work, Mr. Kessler always says, but with a proud grin.

Two sets of twins, he'd like to see anyone compete with that. The twins are six and seven years old. Mrs. Darling can't stand them. She calls them the buy-one-get-one-free kids.

She put the bread sticks into a glass and placed it on the table next to the whole wheat crackers. She turned the television on. We always watch the news before we start on the movies: first the local evening news from Berlin, then the national news. Mrs. Darling is crazy about one of the newscasters on the local news. He's got brown eyes like a teddy bear and his name is Peter Duffel and Mrs. Darling thinks he's fantastic. The last time she came around for a drop of whiskey with Mom she said she thought he was gorgeous.

Today Peter Duffel's beautiful brown eyes looked very serious because the evening news was about Mr. 2000 and the child from Lichtenberg who had been set free. The parents didn't want to give any interviews, so they were showing photos of the other children, whose pictures every Berliner knew from the newspaper and the TV: two boys and two girls, only one of them older than seven. All of them were smiling in their photos, except for little Sophia. Her photo was slightly blurry, but you could still see how close together her eyes were in her flat moon face. Her lips were narrow and almost as pale as her thin eyebrows, her stringy blonde hair hung down over her shoulders, and she was wearing a wrinkled, dark pink T-shirt with a big red splat of strawberry jam or something like that on it. She looked like someone who would get laughed at or teased on the school playground. Sophia was

Mr. 2000's second victim and I felt more sorry for her than for anybody else. I know what it's like when other people are always making fun of you for being different.

The newscaster explained that there was still no sign of the kidnapper and then the news moved on to politics. Next to me, Mrs. Darling made a snorting noise.

"I wish I had that man's address."

"Peter Duffel's?" I could remember his name because it flashed up on the screen regularly. Otherwise my memory for names was down the drain.

"No, the address of the kidnapper." Mrs. Darling pushed half a tomato into her mouth. "There are times when I'd like to send him a personal invitation to come and collect those Kessler kids. Nobody'd miss 'em, if you ask me." She snorted again. "Those buy-one-get-one-free kids are the worst things to have ever lived in this building!"

Mrs. Darling pushed a pickled onion down after her half tomato. She made little crunches as she chewed on it. Then she licked her fingers.

"I think Mr. Fitz is worse."

She waved away the thought and fished out a few bread sticks.

"Nah, he's just putting it on. Another cracker, Rico?"

PUTTING IT ON: Pretending. You'd think you could use one simple word in the first place instead of three confusing ones.

I took a whole wheat cracker and a pickled onion. Mrs. Darling chewed her bread sticks, then suddenly she grabbed the remote control and turned down the sound on the television. They were showing pictures of the cathedral and a couple of cranes, but I couldn't hear what was going on. Quiet spread through the living room. Mrs. Darling looked straight ahead with slightly teary eyes and didn't move again. I looked at her out of the corner of my eye, chewing my cracker and onion carefully. It's always a bit creepy when she has one of her gray days.

"What?" said Mrs. Darling after a while, reluctantly, without turning her head in my direction.

"Maybe you should go out sometimes," I said.

"Is that your idea or your mother's?"

"Mine."

It was Mom's idea. But I'm not such a nitwit that I don't know why people have gray days. You have to be careful as a child proddity not to say things you haven't thought up yourself, though. Otherwise, just like that, people start thinking you're a liar and actually quite smart after all and then they start giving you math problems to do and other stuff. Anyway, you get gray days because you're lonely, and you won't meet other people unless you go out or find somebody on the Internet. I've got no idea how old Mrs. Darling is, almost certainly nearly fifty. But there has to be somebody out there who likes eating wheat crackers, too. In any case, no man has turned up at the butcher's counter for her yet.

The local news was over. Peter Duffel disappeared. Mrs. Darling pressed the OFF button on the remote control firmly. The screen went black, then the pink logo of the DVD player appeared.

"We're watching a murder mystery," said Mrs. Darling as she pushed herself up from the sofa and went over to the cupboard with the film collection. "Miss Marple."

This time I did cheer out loud.

Later, when I was back home lying in bed, I couldn't fall asleep. Part of it was Miss Marple's fault. I always get really nervous when I watch one of her murder mysteries because I'm afraid that something will happen to her. I get so worked up that I always forget I've seen the movie before and that she survived every other time.

Part of the problem was that it was a full moon. It lit the dark, dull windows of the empty apartments in the building behind ours. Old curtains were still hanging in many of them. It's just my luck that it's the third floor that I can see especially well from my bed. That's where Miss Friedmann killed herself. Miss Friedmann was an old lady. One day she got lung cancer and didn't want to go to the hospital. She turned on the gas, lit a final cigarette, and waited a while. Then, *KA-BOOM!*

At first they thought the building hadn't been damaged all that much by the explosion. The apartments where everything was smashed got new windows and stuff, but when they looked at the stairway, they realized the explosion had left cracks in the walls of the fourth and fifth floors. The whole place was in danger of collapse and everybody who lived there had to move out.

The windows in the stairway were boarded up, the door in the yard that led to the apartment building behind ours got a big new security lock, and since then the various owners of the apartments have been fighting over who should pay to have it rebuilt.

That was years and years ago. But Miss Friedmann has been haunting her old rooms since then. That's what the superintendent, Mr. Mommsen, told me right after we moved in. He thinks her ghost is still looking for an ashtray in her old apartment.

Something makes me look over there, whether I want to or not. I've often thought of asking Mom to put up curtains or blinds, but then she might think I was a softy. Sometimes I think I can see even more shadowy shadows behind the shadows in Miss Friedmann's apartment, flitting through the empty rooms. I know I'm just imagining the shadowier shadows, but that doesn't make it easier. Especially when you really have to go to the bathroom but aren't brave enough to get up—and I've never been brave enough when Mom is at work at night and I'm alone in the apartment. I haven't wet the bed for a long time, but if I watch the shadowier shadows flitting around for longer than a minute I just might. That's why I usually pull the blanket over my head before going to sleep.

Just like today.

Under the blanket I thought about Oscar and whether I would ever see him again. Then I fell asleep.

SUNDAY
the summer break diary

I've taken most of Sunday to write down Saturday. But that's OK; I had nothing else to do because Mom was asleep all day. She stays at the club longer than usual on weekends. She didn't come home until ten in the morning and fell into bed right away. Which is why she didn't notice that I was sitting at the computer all day. If my experiment goes wrong, then at least she won't be disappointed.

All this writing was my teacher's idea. That was the reason I had to go and see him on Saturday, even though it was already summer vacation. It started with a story about the canal that I wrote two weeks ago.

The canal flows almost right behind 93 Dieffe Street. You can sit very comfortably on the bank under the giant weeping willows or just on the grass in between all the other people. You can look out over the shining water or tease the paddling swans. Now and then a boat with tourists passes by and you can wave at them. They wave back very excitedly, as though they've never seen a boy sitting on a canal bank before. It's all in the story.

Mr. Meyer said he was extremely impressed by my story—that's why he wanted to talk to me about it again.

"Your spelling is hair-raising, Rico," he said. "But there's something about the way you write. You're a good storyteller—leaving aside the long part about the North Sea."

Mr. Meyer meant my favorite part, where I imagined how it would feel to be a dead body floating in a canal. Imagine it's winter and you've just broken through the ice. The current carries you under the blue-black ice from the canal into the Spree River. I looked at the map of Germany to see where you would go from there: The Spree flows into the Havel River and the Havel flows into the Elbe River and the Elbe flows into the North Sea and the North Sea belongs to the Atlantic. So if you drown in the canal, it's really quite a trip. You get to go on a fantastic journey down three rivers, one sea, and finally into the ocean, unless, of course, you get caught in a ship's propeller and get totally chopped up, which would be annoying.

Mr. Meyer had a strange look on his face. "Are you worried about Mr. 2000? Does it frighten you, all this stuff with the kidnappings?"

So it *was* about the chopped up dead body. I shook my head. I had been thinking about somebody else while I was writing, not about the kidnapper, but that was none of Mr. Meyer's business.

He nodded and looked at the wall with all the photos of his kids and his wife and his dog and his motorcycle, which is nowhere near as nice as Bert's.

"I've been thinking," he said. "What would you say to keeping a diary? About your summer vacation? The things you think about, the things you do . . . Are you and your mom going away anywhere?"

"No. Is this homework?"

"Let's put it like this: If you give it a good try, I'll let you off some other homework assignments after school starts again."

That sounded good.

"How much am I supposed to write?"

"Let's say . . . I'll be happy with three pages. If you manage six, I'll throw in a bonus."

"What's that?"

"An extra reward."

That sounded even better. Even so, I was a bit nervous. Six pages is a lot.

"And the spelling mistakes?" I asked suspiciously.

"Don't worry about that. Don't you have a computer at home?"

"Mom's got one. From eBay."

Mom not only gets rid of her plastic handbags from bingo on eBay, she also buys cheap stuff there, like clothes.

"Does the computer have a word-processing program with an auto-correct function?"

"What does auto-correct mean?"

"It's like a built-in teacher."

BUILT-IN TEACHER FUNCTION: *Now and again somebody explains a word and then you're even more confused. In the beginning, anyway. With auto-correct, for example, you might well be asking yourself how a teacher can possibly live inside a computer.*

Sometimes Mr. Meyer puts together extralong words and sentences just to annoy us. If I'm having a bad day, I get worked up and then the lottery machine starts up. But today I wasn't going to get annoyed. It was summer vacation. And besides, I have to admit, I was pretty excited by his idea. A diary . . .

It took a while, but then I sorted out all his words and understood them. When Mom bought our computer, a word-processing program and a lot of other stuff came with it for free. Mom uses it now and then to write letters. I nodded.

"Good," said Mr. Meyer. "Because a program like that corrects your spelling mistakes automatically."

I was astounded. "Really?"

"Really. But do me a favor and at least look at some of the worst mistakes. Maybe you'll learn something."

Was he off his rocker? If I looked at each mistake one by one, the lottery balls would go crazy.

"Deal?" said Mr. Meyer.

"Deal."

He grinned and raised his hand. "Give me five."

I pushed my chair back, stood up, quickly said good-bye, and left. If he was about to move on to math, that would ruin everything.

Well, that's it up until now. And I've written more than six pages. So I can take a break. Writing is hard work. But I'll get my bonus! Mr. Meyer will be amazed.

The automatic-correction thing isn't all that great, though. A few pages back I'd written a word the wrong way, *swones* instead of *swans*. The program suggested the following sentence: *You can look out over the shining water or tease the paddling scones.*

MONDAY
the new neighbor

Around lunchtime there was a knock at the front door. Mom had just got up and shuffled past my room. I heard her swooshing around in the kitchen, making coffee.

"Can you answer?" she called.

I'd never seen the man at the door before. He was tall and thin with short black hair, electric blue eyes, and a small scar on his chin. He looked like an actor.

"Hello!" He smiled and stretched out his hand. "I thought it was time I came by and introduced myself. I moved in a few days ago, upstairs on the fourth floor. I'm Simon Westhaven."

I didn't answer. I stared at the scar on his chin, then at his outstretched hand, then back at his chin again, and wished he was just called Mr. Haven. A small needle on a compass was spinning crazily in front of my eyes—west, east, west, east. I turned red and began to sweat. That's the problem with the lottery balls: They start to roll around whether it's a good time or not. I could hear them clacking against the inside of my skull.

Mr. Haven was still wearing a friendly smile, but there

were suddenly two tiny question marks in his eyes, as though he'd never seen a boy sweating so badly before. His hand was still hanging in the air in front of me. He must have thought I was crazy. I thought I'd better pull myself together. A name with a single compass point in it shouldn't be that difficult, even for a child proddity like me.

"Who is it?" Mom called from the kitchen.

"Mr. Easthaven," I yelled back. "The new neighbor from the fourth floor."

Clack, clack, clacker-dee-clack.

"I can always come back . . . ," Mr. Haven began, and then his voice seeped away like the rain in one of our gutters. He looked over my shoulder with wide eyes. I turned around.

Mom had come into the hallway in her bare feet. She was fiddling around with her freshly dyed strawberry-blonde hair, trying to tie it into a ponytail at the neck. She looked very pretty, but I would have preferred it if she'd been wearing more than a man's shirt to come to the door—it was so short you could see her panties!

Mr. Haven looked her up and down very quickly without moving his head. His cheeks started to turn red. If he begins to sweat, too, that'll be that, I thought.

"Just a second," Mom said as though he was only the postman, and slipped into the bathroom. There was a splashing of water. You could hear her gargling.

"She's using mouthwash," I whispered to Mr. Haven.

He nodded in a friendly way and pretended to be looking ·

around our beautiful hallway, but he kept glancing at me strangely. Seconds later Mom came out of the bathroom in her Japanese robe with the painted symbols on it. We sometimes guess at what they might mean—*Good Morning*, maybe, or *Peace on Earth* or *Eat More Vegetables!*

"Sorry," she murmured, standing in front of Mr. Haven before finally grabbing his outstretched hand. "Tanja Doretti." She smiled. "At least I think so. I'm not quite awake yet."

"Simon Westhaven. I hope I haven't—"

"Not at all. Come on in." She turned around and headed toward the kitchen. "Coffee?" she asked over her shoulder. "I've just put the machine on. I'm not much use before I've had my first cup."

I once watched a film with Mrs. Darling about a famous Greek hero . . . his name began with O and he was in a wooden horse in a war and then he sailed around and about on his ship for years to get back to his wife. She'd stayed at home, where she was being chased by a thousand men who all were in love with her. O clearly didn't know this, otherwise he might have got a bit more of a move on. Instead he kept getting lost in his boat and had all these crazy adventures, but in the end he finally got back to his wife and got rid of all the other guys with bows and arrows, etc. What a cool story!

Anyway, at some point during one of the journeys when he got lost in the middle of a storm out at sea, O sailed past an island, and there were singing ladies there, some kind of mermaids. Anybody who heard them went completely crazy and tried to reach them, and a few of O's men jumped into the water and drowned gruesomely. One of the sailors said the ladies' voices were like honey and milk, even though Mrs. Darling didn't think their warbling was all that great. She almost changed the channel to watch the late-night lotto drawing, but she really wanted to know what would happen to O's wife. Anyway, O got the other sailors to tie him to the mast and that's how he escaped with his life.

Nobody had tied up Mr. Haven. He followed Mom into the kitchen as though she'd just sung him a beautiful song, and he looked almost exactly the same as when O couldn't escape from the ship's mast. Mom pointed to a chair and placed two cups on the table without saying a word. The coffee machine bubbled away. I sat down across from Mr. Haven. He looked much more handsome than the actor who'd played O. And he looked really at home in our kitchen.

"Are you married?" I said.

He started to grin and shook his head. His teeth were very clean and white.

"Do you have a girlfriend?"

"Rico!" hissed Mom.

"Don't worry." Mr. Haven grinned without shifting his gaze from me. He didn't answer the question, but I liked him, anyway. I like Mr. Kirk from the third floor as well, or at least the way he looks. But he's normally pretty grumpy. He probably doesn't like children all that much. And Mr. Kirk would never marry Mom; he's not all that into women.

"We're going to bingo tomorrow night," I said. "At the Gray Bumblebees. Do you want to come?"

"Rico, go to your room," Mom ordered. "Please!"

"Bingo?" Mr. Haven said. "I've never . . . Isn't that for retirees?"

"Yes, but there's a spare place because one of them has just died. Except nobody noticed. And Mom almost always wins, sometimes even with my card!"

Even the lamest old lady can cross off the numbers on her bingo card faster than I can. But it's fun all the same.

"Frederico!" Mom said in a stern voice. "Off with you!"

It's always serious when she uses my full name. I wondered what the problem was. It was just getting interesting between her and Mr. Haven—the two of them about to have coffee together, etc. Who knew what they would talk about, and knowing Mom she'd probably say the wrong thing. I could have helped her because I know from Mrs. Darling's romantic movies exactly what you're supposed to say so that it all works out, but I couldn't do anything from my room. So I would miss the whole thing, unless, of course—

"And if you listen in, I'll auction you off on eBay! I want to hear your door close behind you."

Mom finally poured Mr. Haven some coffee. Mr. Haven looked at me, raised both his hands, shrugged his shoulders, and made a funny face. No help to be had from him, then. He probably really wanted to be left alone with Mom.

Honestly!

I ran to my room really fast and banged my door shut behind me. Mom can't stand it when I do that, but she had nobody to blame but herself. Ten minutes later I heard Mr. Haven saying good-bye in the hallway. I crept to the door and listened. He said thank you for the coffee and all that, but nothing along the lines of see you tomorrow evening at bingo.

Oh well!

The front door opened and closed. I shot straight out into the hallway, past Mom, who isn't used to me being so speedy. I really wanted to say good-bye to Mr. Haven. That much had to be allowed. So I opened the door, rushed out into the stairway, and—

It was probably the biggest collision 93 Dieffe Street has ever seen. What a mess! In front of our door three men had run into one another, and because I had Mr. Haven on the brain, it took me a few seconds to take the other two in. One of them was Mr. Marrak, who was trying to get up the stairs with all of today's and yesterday's mail, or at least half of it, because the rest was scattered across the floor. The other one was Mr. Kirk, who was trying to get down the stairs. At the very moment Mr. Haven had walked out of our door, the other two must have met on the landing, and now all three were tangled up in a big knot. There was a jangling and a clattering while Mr. Marrak tried to collect his letters. He has his own security business, so he always carries a big bunch of keys on the belt of his red uniform, which has a small golden safe embroidered on it. Very fancy.

Mr. Kirk clasped at his own shirt with one hand and stared wide-eyed at Mr. Haven. Mr. Haven then turned helplessly from one direction to the other, and all of them were muttering: sorry, I wasn't looking, never mind, it's not a big deal, I was in such a rush, but nothing serious happened—who does that child belong to?

Something small had almost got lost in the general chaos. It looked all three men up and down through a visor. Then it called out in horror, "If I hadn't had my helmet on, I'd be dead by now!"

Mom was completely flabbergasted that somebody had come to visit me. She's always complaining that I don't have any friends. Now I had one. Admittedly, he was a bit small and probably also on the young side, but Mom didn't seem all that bothered. She was much more interested in Oscar's blue motorcycle helmet.

"Since when do people wear things like that to ride a bicycle?" she said.

She was leaning against the kitchen stove, sipping from the coffee cup she held in her hands. Mr. Haven's cup was standing all by itself between Oscar and me on the table, only half drunk.

"I don't have a bicycle," Oscar said. His voice sounded muffled, because the visor on his helmet was still pushed down.

"I bet you don't have a motorcycle, either."

Oscar looked at her as though she wasn't all there, brains-wise. But he did push up his visor. You still couldn't see his whole mouth, just the top row of his large white teeth.

"It's dangerous without a helmet," he explained, as though Mom was the child and he was the adult. "Accidents happen all the time."

"Not in my kitchen they don't, young man!" Mom sounded almost insulted. "I'm sure Rico will confirm that for you."

I wrinkled my forehead. "But I did bang my head on the fridge last week."

"That wasn't an accident," Mom said firmly. "You came out of the hall too fast and ran into the open door."

Oscar didn't feel comfortable with Mom there, I could tell. He peered out from under his helmet like a tortoise. He was wearing a different shirt today, but the bright red airplane with the broken wing was pinned just above his heart. His little fingers were tapping on the table nervously, *rap tee-tap*. Oscar was probably afraid that Mom would think he was rude and demand that he take off his helmet.

He wasn't completely wrong about that, but not com-pletely right, either. Mom can deal with strange people. Her first rule is, never put pressure on anyone if they don't want to do something. At least not with words. But she looks. She looks at people for so long they can't take it anymore and finally give in.

She was looking at Oscar now the way a scientist would

look at a completely new type of plant she'd just discovered. I was wondering myself what Oscar looked like under his helmet. Maybe he wasn't actually afraid of accidents. Maybe he had two funny ears and was ashamed of them. Or no ears at all—like one of Mr. 2000's victims who hadn't raised enough ransom money.

Oscar's fingers got slower and slower, and then they stopped their tapping. He raised his head, looked Mom right in the eyes, and said, "You can stare at me as long as you like. I don't care. But I'll stare back."

And that's what he did. For the first time I noticed how green his eyes were. They really gleamed. Not nastily or angrily. They were gleaming because Oscar enjoyed staring back. At that moment I was really jealous of him being a child prodigy. Whenever Mom stares at me, I always look straight at the floor, as though something really interesting is going on down there, like colorful ants running around or a fire on the carpet. Till I saw Oscar I'd never thought of staring back.

I wondered which one of them would win. Mom was my mom so I probably should have taken her side. She was good at staring and didn't bat an eyelid. But Oscar was just a little kid and I thought the whole staring contest was a bit unfair. Either Mom thought that, too, or she lost interest.

Whichever it was, she suddenly said, "I need new toenails."

Oscar and I both looked at her toenails. There was a tiny dolphin on each one; the two little toes were the only places too small for them to fit.

"What do you want to put on them instead?" Oscar said. It sounded like a peace offering.

Mom shrugged. "Not sure. Maybe some other kind of fish."

She put her coffee cup down on the sink, pulled her Japanese robe around her, and went out of the kitchen. Oscar waited until she was out of earshot, then he said quietly in my direction, "Dolphins aren't fish."

"She likes you," I said.

He shook his head. "She doesn't know if she likes me yet. She thinks I'm funny because of the helmet." He pulled the visor back down. His voice sounded muffled again. "Every year almost forty thousand children in Germany die in accidents. Almost a third of them are passengers in cars. Almost forty percent are on bikes. And twenty-five percent are pedestrians."

Math! I've already told you it's not my strong point.

"Most of them are knocked down on their way to school and while playing in the afternoon," Oscar murmured darkly. "Most of the cyclists are killed because they're using the wrong lane. Most of the pedestrians because they run across the street without looking. I always look. Always!"

I am learning that one of the big differences between Oscar and me is that I am in a good mood nearly all the time, but I don't know very much, whereas Oscar knows all kinds of strange things, but he is always expecting the worst. That's probably what happens when you're very smart—you can't just think of nice things, you have to think of terrible things, too.

I jumped up. I'd had an idea. "I'll show you something," I said. "It's not dangerous at all and it's great!"

"What is it?"

"Wait, I have to ask Mom something first."

I burst into the living room—today really was a fast day! Mom was curled up on our thinking chair in front of the windowsill. She was looking out the window. She was miles away. There wasn't a trace of nail polish or new stickers for her toes. She'd probably lied and just wanted some peace and quiet.

"What do you think of him?" I whispered.

She turned to me and wrinkled her nose. "I think he's a bit weird. Where did you dig him up? I've never seen a kid with a crash helmet. . . ."

"I don't mean Oscar. I mean Mr. Haven."

"Oh . . ." Suddenly she looked really tired, as though she hadn't slept for a week. Her eyes closed slowly and then opened again and then she talked, slowly and firmly.

"Rico, Listen. I know you would really like a father. And I wish for both of our sakes that there was one here, believe me! But that doesn't mean I'm going to fall for every man you think might fit the job."

Oh well, so she thought Mr. Haven was awful. Maybe it had something to do with her job in the nightclub. She was always being bothered by some guy or other. Maybe she

49

just didn't want to do the same stuff at home. But if Mom wasn't careful, she might suddenly find herself having a gray day. Up until now she had never brought a boyfriend home, even though she met loads of men at work, a lot more than Mrs. Darling did behind the meat counter. One of them had to be right.

"OK. But what do you think of him? Please!" It was important to me that she liked Mr. Haven, even if it was only a little bit. *I* liked him.

"Simon Westhaven." She thought hard. "Well, I . . . I'd say he's far and away the hottest thing I've met in my entire life."

I wanted to be excited, for her and for me. But Mom just looked out the window again. Now she not only looked tired but a little sad, too, and even though she was right in front of me, she seemed far, far away, like a lonely speck on the horizon. Sometimes I don't understand my mom at all.

HORIZON: The spot right at the back of the world where earth and sky meet. Or is it the sea and the sky? It can't be the earth and the sea, that would have to be vertical, and then it would almost certainly be called something else. Like the searizon.

MONDAY AGAIN
up on the roof

I took Oscar out of our apartment. The knot of men had untangled itself and there was nobody else to be seen. As I pulled the door shut behind me, I had a thought. "Who let you into the building, Oscar?"

His visor was up again. He took a deep breath, as though he had been expecting the question for ages and could now finally, finally give an answer. "Nobody. The front door was open!" he let out in disgust. "Your neighbors should be more careful. Anybody could come in! Murderers, burglars, drunks who pee in the hallway. How can they be so careless?!"

I shrugged. I had left the door to the building open a few times myself. It has a little hook at the back that clicks into a holder on the wall if you push it open hard. Not a big deal, unless your name is Oscar. In Oscar's life everything is dangerous—or at least he seems to think so.

"And how did you know which bell to ring?"

"From the list of names at the entrance." His voice had gone all squeaky and rang up the stairs in front of us like a siren. "It was *open*!"

"Yes, all right, I heard you the first time." I was becoming nervous. If he kept ranting on like that, we'd bump into Mr. Fitz as well. I jumped up the stairs. "So, how did you figure out my name?"

He quickly stumbled after me on his short legs, and finally he calmed down a little. "You said your father was Italian. Doretti is the only name on the list of names next to the door-bells that sounds Italian."

I was annoyed I hadn't thought of that myself; Oscar was very detectivey.

"Do you know Miss Marple?" I asked.

"No. Does she live here, too?"

Ha! Now I could show him! Everybody knows the Miss Marple movies! But maybe child prodigies don't watch television; they just appear on it, rattling off prime numbers on talent shows and stuff. I swallowed my not-very-nice-but-very-funny comment. If you like somebody, you shouldn't make fun of them, and Oscar could probably make fun of me ten times better than I could make fun of him, and he'd be able to find one hundred times more chances to do it. That made me think about little Sophia with her moon face and the big, fat strawberry stain on her creased T-shirt—I bet she was really badly made fun of at her school.

"Don't run so fast!" Oscar wheezed. He was having difficulty keeping up. If his visor had been shut, it would have steamed up from all his breath. "Where are you taking me?"

Reluctantly I slowed down a little. We'd almost arrived at the fourth floor—Mr. Fitz's territory. And Mr. Fitz gets grumpy when it gets noisy on the staircase. He hates noise even more than Mrs. Darling does.

"We're going up to the fifth floor," I said in a low voice.

"What's up there?"

"The fifth floor, of course."

"I mean, what are we going to *do* up there?"

I grinned. "You'll see. I hope you don't get dizzy."

"Dizzy?" shrieked Oscar. He sounded like a wailing siren. "You're not taking me *up on the roof*?"

The next second, a door flew open and a wave of stinkiness hit us. Mr. Fitz was standing before us in his tattered striped pajamas as if he'd just escaped from a thrift store. He hadn't shaved since I saw him on Saturday, or combed his hair, and he looked like a mop that had had an electric shock.

"Could you possibly be any louder?" he thundered. "I've got a heart condition. What's all this noise about—" He stopped suddenly and stared in surprise at Oscar, who was at least ten feet smaller than he was. Oscar quickly snapped his visor into place and stared back.

"What kind of strange creature are you?" said Mr. Fitz.

No reply.

"Can't you talk?" Mr. Fitz tapped on the helmet three times with his finger. "Hello? I asked you a question."

"You stink!" Oscar suddenly shouted through the visor.

53

"In developing countries, lack of hygiene is one of the biggest causes of illness! We have warm running water and soap. And you should use it."

Mr. Fitz eyed him as if he were an irritating insect he was about to squash with the palm of his hand. His gaze moved from Oscar's helmet to the bright red airplane on his shirt and back to the helmet. I held my breath.

"Who are you?" Mr. Fitz finally growled.

"Oscar. Who are you?"

"None of your business. And now buzz off before I rip your heads off and play football with them!"

That was the worst thing I had ever heard! Mr. Fitz spun around and the door went *SLAM!* Oscar took two quick steps forward, stretched out one hand, and pressed the bell firmly.

"Don't do that!" I hissed. "He'll make mincemeat out of us if we annoy him again!" Either that or he really would rip our heads off.

"The bell's broken," Oscar snorted as if he hadn't heard me. He hammered on the door as though he wanted to break it down.

"What are you doing?" I grabbed his wrist and pulled him away. I was beginning to get angry, too.

"He's rude!" Oscar pushed up his visor. His face had turned as red as a tomato. "I'm not being treated like that just because I'm a child!"

"That's Mr. Fitz. It's just the way he is. He probably doesn't mean it."

I was absolutely certain that Mr. Fitz did mean it, but Oscar was angry enough already.

"And I'm not a strange creature!" he roared through the closed door.

"He says that to everybody. You can't get upset about it," I urged. "Now come on!"

He followed me in the end. But as we were taking the last set of stairs up to the fifth floor, he kept turning around as though he expected Mr. Fitz to pop up again and chase after us. And he kept his right hand clenched in a fist until I had let us into the Kaminsky-Kowalskys' apartment.

Before the KKs zoomed off on vacation last Friday, they asked me if I'd water their houseplants and the flowers on the roof terrace for a little bit of pocket money. Of course, I said. There was a new baseball cap I really wanted, although I probably won't buy it now after all. I've decided to put all my money in my piggy bank, just in case Mom has to buy the biggest possible piece of me from Mr. 2000.

When you enter the KKs' apartment, you go through a large, open hallway into an even bigger living room and kitchen. There's a nice view from the windows over the flat-roofed hospital and the streets, all the way over to the airport. A narrow staircase leads directly up from the kitchen to the roof terrace. There's nothing else to see, though. They've closed off all the other rooms, even fat Freddy's, the one who always makes fun of me when nobody else is there. They probably think I'd go nosing around. They're so suspicious. Before they went away they put all of their houseplants on the kitchen table for watering. I steered Oscar past the table and up the stairs in front of me. He didn't even want to look around.

The roof terrace is the shape of a beach towel. When you go out of the terrace door, you can go over to the railing and look down into the backyard, or you can go to the other side and look down onto Dieffe Street. There are a few flowerpots and buckets with green stuff growing out of them. Most of the space is taken up by wooden chairs, a table, and a bench, and if you have a cushion to put under your rear end and a comic and a Coke, it's a nice place to sit. You can hear all the noises of the city, a never-ending, muffled humming, buzzing, and hissing. And the view is phenomenal.

PHENOMENAL: Amazing, fantastic, unique, really cool.
I know this word already. But I'm writing it down here to
show that I know some long words, too.

If you stand in the middle of the roof terrace, stretch out your arms, and turn around in a circle, you can look out over Berlin in every direction. You can see hundreds of rooftops and the tops of thousands of green trees, all kinds of church towers, the television tower on Alexander Square, and the skyscrapers on Potsdam Square. In the sky above there's almost always an airplane that has taken off from one of the city's airports, or is landing. If you turn a little faster, all of these sights blur into one and you get dizzy. And if you turn *really* fast, you'll probably zoom over one of the railings with a few of the flowerpots and race them to the bottom where you'll burst like a ripe tomato. Real blood sauce and all the rest. Which is why I've never tried to go really fast. I'm not a complete idiot.

Oscar was not one bit impressed by any of it. He pressed his back to the terrace door and what you could see of his face through the helmet was very pale.

Even his voice was pale somehow. But it was angry at the same time.

"You said it would be great up here, not dangerous!"

"It is."

I was giving up all hope of him taking off his helmet. What was the matter with him? I'd expected a person who only thought about squashed bicyclists and run-over pedestrians to be happy with a change of scene. And it wasn't dangerous up here—unless, of course, an airplane plopped down on the building. I thought about asking Oscar how much he knew about airplane crashes, but that probably wasn't a good idea.

"I've never been up on a roof," he said in a whiny voice.

I pointed to the railing that looked out over Dieffe Street. "You haven't even been up to the edge. You can hold on to the railing."

"I can swim," he groaned, "but I still wouldn't jump into a pool full of piranhas."

"What are piranhas?"

"Predatory fish with very sharp teeth from the *Serrasalmus* family. They live in the tropical freshwater of South America. They can rip an injured animal or a human to shreds in a few seconds."

All right, then. If I ever met one of the *Serra*-whatsit family, I would know where I stood. But . . .

"Are you terrified of everything?" I asked.

"I'm not terrified. I'm being cautious."

I should have brought some Coke or lemonade. Maybe then Oscar would have felt more comfortable up here. I didn't want to run back down to the second floor, and the KKs' fridge, which I had peeked into by chance, was empty. Completely cleared out. How mean was that?!

"I'm just being cautious," Oscar repeated quietly. "It's the instinct for self-preservation. You know—keeping yourself alive."

I looked at him helplessly. I had brought him up here for a reason. I was starting to suspect he wouldn't be all that excited about my great idea, but seeing as we were up here already, I could at least try.

I pointed to the fold-up screen made of thick, tightly woven bamboo canes that separated the KKs' roof terrace from the one next door.

"Would you like to look through the petition?"

"It's called a partition."

"I know. I was just testing."

Thank goodness he didn't look at me; otherwise he would have noticed right away that I'd turned bright red. Just then I would have liked to borrow his helmet.

PARTITION: Easily confused with a letter of complaint signed by lots of people, which is also a difficult word to learn. A partition is like a wall that protects you from drafts and nosy neighbors.

"What's behind there?" said Oscar.

"Mr. Marrak's roof terrace."

"Who?"

"One of the three men you bumped into on the staircase. The one in the red uniform with the golden safe on it. He has his own business." I took a deep breath without him noticing. "Alarms, Safes, and Locks: Sales, Service, and Installation."

I said the sentence calmly, as if I were picking a daisy from a meadow, but really I had almost fainted with the effort. Now I was bursting with pride because I hadn't made a single mistake. Mr. Marrak had once given me one of his business cards. I had studied it at least ten times a day every day for a week and learned it all by heart so that I could impress somebody one day. I never dreamed that it would be smarty-pants Oscar.

But all Oscar said was, "I see."

Honestly! He can really ruin your good mood. On the other hand I should have known that long, complicated things are easy as pie for a child prodigy. How do they manage to know so much and remember new things right away? And what *don't* they know?

"How far away from the earth is the moon?" I asked.

"Just under two hundred and forty thousand miles."

Aha! His answer came as quick as a shot, but *just under* is not quite the same as *all the way there*, and before you know it you'd end up landing on Mars, Jupiter, or Uranus, instead of on the moon.

URANUS: On photos it's as blue as Oscar's crash helmet. At first I wrote YURANUS, but it seems that the automatic-correction thing works after all.

"The exact average distance," said Oscar next to me slowly, "is two hundred and thirty-eight thousand, eight hundred and fifty-five miles."

OK, one–nil to Oscar. But I didn't want to give up completely. "But you had to think about it, didn't you?"

"I thought you wanted to know how far the moon is from the earth today. But to know that we would first have to ascertain the daily parallax; and you can only do that if—"

"Don't worry about it." I gave up. "So, do you want to look at the other roof terrace or not?"

"Why?"

"Because I want to show you something. It's not one bit dangerous!" I added quickly before he could start the siren thing again. "We just have to be a little careful because Mr. Marrak just got home. He might want to lie on his terrace in this nice weather."

Finally Oscar let go of the door and came to join me by the partition. He shoved right up next to me and helped me push the bamboo canes apart so we could see through to the other side. Mr. Marrak's roof terrace is a lot larger than the KKs'. There are more plants, fancier furniture, and the floor is made of thick, beautifully streaked wooden planks, much better than the KKs' red-brown tiles.

"Nice," whispered Oscar. His fingers were short and his nails were tiny and bitten. Not even the smallest of Mom's nail stickers would have fit onto them.

"What's that over there, that house-shaped thing with the pointed roof?" he said. "The one right at the back on the left?"

"Which one is left again?"

I almost bit my tongue. I didn't mean to ask that. It just slipped out. I could see the stupid little house right in front of me, or its roof at least, because the entrance was hidden on both sides by more bamboo.

But Oscar simply said, "Left is where you see the little roof."

"Of course. I knew that. It's the top of the staircase of the next building—the one behind this one. Mr. Marrak let me peek in once when I was in his apartment. You used to be able to get into it from here, but you can't anymore. The door to the little house is locked because there was a gas explosion. Since then the building's been condensed."

Oscar turned his head toward me with a jerk. He almost sliced off my ear with his open visor. "It's been what?"

"Condensed. If you hear so badly under your funny helmet—"

"It's *condemned*, not *condensed*."

"That's what I said."

"You didn't."

"I did."

"You did!"

"I didn't!"

Oscar wrinkled his nose triumphantly. "You see."

Something had gone wrong in all the fast words, but I didn't have time to think about what it was.

"Oh, never mind!" I pointed to the little house with the locked door. "Anyway, that's where we're going, in there."

"Into the building that's been condemned?"

I nodded.

"Now you've really gone crazy. If it's condemned, that means it could be about to fall down!"

Flippin' heck! All I wanted was to see for myself that there were no shadowier shadows. And no Miss Friedmann. With Oscar by my side it wouldn't be scary, it would just be the two of us on a big adventure.

"And the building is just as locked up as that little house

over there"—Oscar gestured at the pointy roof—"so there's absolutely no chance. What do you think I am, a burglar?"

"I thought we could ask Mr. Marrak for a key. He could come with us. We could see if there's anything still lying around in the empty apartments." That was my last useless attempt. "A few cool old things. That kind of stuff."

"Forget it."

He wouldn't change his mind and that made me annoyed. "Are you scared again?" I said, facing up to him.

"It's got nothing to do with being scared. It's about being sensible."

"So you *are* scared again!"

"You're a real pain in the neck, do you know that?" said Oscar with a sigh. He took a deep breath and went over to the railing from which you can look down into the backyard. Carefully he leaned over it, but only a little bit. He even stood on his tiptoes and began to rock gently, as though he were listening to music no one else could hear.

When I saw him standing there, something strange happened. I thought of Molly One and Molly Two. Molly One was my fifth birthday present from Mom. I'd never seen a hamster before, or I might have seen one but forgotten. In any case, I thought Molly was great. She waddled around and sniffed the air with her tiny pink nose. Mom had put her in a small straw basket and tied a yellow ribbon around her middle.

"There's a cage, of course. I've hidden it in the living room. Hang on one second, love."

I nodded happily and took Molly out of the basket. I'd never held something as small and warm and alive as that before. I pressed her to my chest because I loved her so much, and there was a *crack*.

I got Molly Two a week later because I couldn't stop crying. She moved into the cage meant for Molly One. Mom and I had buried Molly One in a small park. I can't remember its name. I hope she's OK there.

Molly Two was around for a lot longer than Molly One. Mom kept on reminding me that I shouldn't hold her too tightly, so I didn't squeeze this time. But I let her run around in my room until one day she disappeared.

"That's it," Mom said after we'd turned the whole apartment upside down at least three times. "No more hamsters. I think, Frederico, you're not yet ready to take responsibility for a small creature. Sorry. It was my mistake."

Oscar had finished rocking and turned toward me.

"There you go. Happy now?"

"Not bad for starters," I said generously.

"What about you?" He looked at me. "Aren't you afraid of anything?"

"Yes. I'm afraid I could get lost in the city," I admitted. "I can't find my way, you know. With all those lefts and rights and stuff."

"Has that ever happened?"

"Nah, I've never been very far by myself. It wouldn't actually be that bad. Mom says if I ever get lost, I should get in a taxi and let them bring me home. If she's not in, somebody in the building will lend me the money."

"Good idea. And besides getting lost?"

I shook my head. I had to be careful. There was something I was more afraid of than getting lost, and I had already been thinking that I would have to tell Oscar as soon as we became official friends. But I wasn't sure if he really was my official friend already. I would have to check.

"Are you coming back tomorrow?" I asked him.

I felt my face go red with excitement. That was a pretty smart test, I thought. Official friends always have time for each other. They want to have as many adventures together as possible. If Oscar said no . . .

He looked at me carefully, like I was something on a shelf in the supermarket that he wasn't sure he wanted to buy. He scratched his arm. He fingered his airplane badge. He chewed on his lower lip with those large teeth of his.

"Actually," he said, "I've got plans for tomorrow. They could take all day."

My heart almost hit the tiled floor on the KKs' terrace. But only almost. At the last second Oscar changed his mind. "But I can probably do that another time," he said quickly.

I stretched one arm out in relief. "Are we official friends now?"

He placed his little hand into mine. It was really warm. He smiled. "Isn't that what we've been the whole time?"

* * *

I'm sitting here writing. Normally I would have been asleep for a long time by now, but Mom has gone out with Irina and her new toenails—she did put new stickers on after all, small white daisies with really tiny yellow pollen thingies in the middle (I'm not going to look up the word now). And she said I could go to bed whenever I felt like it. It is summer vacation, after all. Now I'm sitting here and I have to write down everything that I'm thinking about so I remember it tomorrow.

First of all I have to say that today was at least half a success. Oscar's my friend now, even if he has a screw loose, and Mom thinks that Mr. Haven is the hottest thing she's ever seen, even though she doesn't want to flirt with him. Flirting is when you go out with somebody; then you fall in love, get married, and make babies. I could tell Mom that I don't mind what order she does that in and then she might see things differently and invite Mr. Haven to bingo tomorrow after all.

Hopefully!

Earlier, I sat in the thinking chair and looked out the window. The moon is still almost full and if you turn your head a bit, you can see it between the branches of those trees with the funny peeling bark. Today the moon is completely orange. It's probably on fire up there just under two hundred and forty thousand miles away. So I was sitting there, thinking about the day, and I suddenly asked myself what was going on this afternoon in the stairway when everybody crashed into each other. I mean, today was Monday! It's normal for

Mr. Marrak to be around at that time of day—he can do what he wants with his time because he has his own business—but what was somebody like Mr. Haven doing at home? He must have some kind of a job, otherwise he couldn't rent such an expensive apartment. Was he on vacation or what? And Mr. Kirk, too—out and about in the middle of the day when he should have been making teeth.

Very strange.

I'm really looking forward to tomorrow! Oscar is coming over and we're going to go for a walk by the canal, even if Oscar doesn't know it yet. It'll be great. If the weather's nice, maybe we'll get ice-cream cones. Nah, we'll get ice-cream cones whatever the weather. And then I'll tell Oscar what my greatest fear is and where it comes from. I'll tell him the story of how my dad died.

TUESDAY
up and down

Sometimes you wake up in the morning, open your eyes, and think of something beautiful right away. It's as though a little sun is rising inside you, making you all warm and bright.

Oscar and I had arranged to meet at ten o'clock. I snuggled up in bed and pictured us walking along the canal together. When I'm alone I only ever go straight over the bridge to school because as soon as I lose sight of things I know, it's over and out. I'd get lost in a supermarket even if it only had one aisle. I'm a hopeless case.

But today Oscar would be with me. We could turn left and right wherever we liked. We could walk far, far down the canal, somewhere I'd never been before. With a child prodigy at your side, far, far away is a piece of cake. Even if you do get lost, your friend can ask somebody the way and he'll remember what people tell him, left and right and all the rest of it. It would be a piece of cake with icing on top!

I saw the wall of the building behind shimmering through the window. There were no shadows from the clouds. It would be a perfect day with Oscar. And this evening I was going to bingo with Mom. Maybe I could persuade her to take Mr. Haven along after all. Or I could ask Mr. Haven if he felt like showing up without an invitation. He could pretend he was looking for his helpless old mother, who got lost while shopping in a supermarket with only one aisle. What if he never found her, the poor lady? What a mystery!

I looked at my Mickey Mouse alarm clock. Almost nine o'clock—I still had an hour. Then again it could also be a quarter to twelve, because sometimes I confuse Mickey's short and long arms, but I never wake up that late, not even on vacation, and I was sure Oscar would have rung the bell if I had overslept.

I jumped out of bed, went to the bathroom, and tiptoed past Mom's bedroom into the kitchen to get a bowl of Crunchy Nut Clusters and a glass of orange juice. Ten minutes later I'd had my breakfast, brushed my teeth, and was dressed and ready to go.

Much too early.

If I'm waiting for something or I don't really know what to do with myself, I sit in the thinking chair in the living room. I can't remember when Mom and I named it the thinking chair, but we really love it. It's big and cozy. Sometimes I need it to calm down the lottery barrel. But it's also great to sit in and read comics and to look out the window at the leaves of the trees moving in the wind. Sometimes sparrows sit in the trees' branches, chirping at each other excitedly. You can think up stories with heroes like O and his wooden horse or you can think about important questions such as whether Miss Marple will ever marry Mr. Stringer. He's her best friend. He's clumsy and too stupid for Miss Marple, but she's got nobody else to fall in love with except the fat stable owner.

Hours later, when Mom got up, I was still sitting in the thinking chair. I'd already jumped up a hundred times, run to the window, and looked out over Dieffe Street. At one point I saw Mr. Marrak leaving the house and walking off, on the way to his car that was parked nearby. But that was it.

No crash helmet anywhere.

No little spot of blue.

No Oscar.

I dragged myself over to Mom in the kitchen, in such a bad mood that I felt as heavy and sad as an elephant. Elephants go into the jungle to die. They go to a place where other elephants have died before them, and before those elephants, other elephants who were looking for a place to die near other dead elephants. A giant elephant graveyard.

Our kitchen was not a graveyard, but I had to go somewhere. I sat at the table and moaned about my bad luck. Mom poured herself a cup of coffee and sat across from me.

"He stood you up, huh?"

I wasn't sure what she meant. Oscar had been standing up when he left the building yesterday, but I couldn't remember if I was standing up or sitting down. That couldn't be what she meant. But instead of saying something, I nodded quickly.

Sometimes I'm embarrassed to show Mom that I don't get things.

"Well, it looks as though both of us are having a bad start to the day," she continued. "I have to go away for two or three days."

And that was that. There were dark shadows under her eyes. Maybe she'd slept badly. I looked at her, waiting. She looked back. She sipped her coffee. Finally she sighed.

"Do you understand, love? I've got to leave this afternoon. That means there won't be any bingo for us this evening."

That means . . . *what?!*

"I'm sorry, Rico! I know how much you were looking forward to it."

Great, no bingo, either! Where was she going? She probably wanted to do a tour of all the hairdressers in the city with her friend Irina to get new hints put in her hair. Well, I was used to being left standing up and all alone. One day Mom would come home after a pipe had burst or something and I would be lying drowned in the hall, next to a letter telling her that I had to repeat the school year. It would serve her right!

"Where are you going?" I asked her grumpily

"Do you remember Uncle Christian?"

Only a little bit. I don't like him at all. Uncle Christian is Mom's older brother; he lives somewhere in Germany down at the bottom and left. A few years ago, before we moved into this apartment, he visited us in Berlin. He and Mom had such a fight that I hid under my bed. He left that same day.

I couldn't remember what he looked like anymore or how his voice sounded.

"Yes, he's not very nice," I said. "What about him?"

"He's not very well. I have to go and see him."

"Why? What's the matter?"

"Cancer."

Everybody knows what cancer is, even Forrest Gump. If Mom was saying such a serious word as though there was nothing to it, then something was wrong. She said *cancer* as cheerfully as Mrs. Darling would say, "A tiny bit more, perhaps?" at the meat counter.

"Will he die?" I asked slowly.

"Yes. He might."

If the train takes a long time, Uncle Christian might be dead when she arrives, then our bingo game will have been canceled for nothing.

"Do you have to go today?" I said.

"Oh for God's sake!" Mom shouted at me just like that. "Do you have to be so self-centered? Can't you think about somebody else for a change?"

SELF-CENTEREDNESS: When you only think about yourself. There's also the opposite thing, when you only think about other people, and if you can do that you're a saint. But saints usually get treated badly and burned at the stake. It's important to find out how to do both so

72

that you get what you want and make other people happy
at the same time.

Mom poured herself another cup of coffee without look-ing at me. She took a sip. She started to cry. It was as though a rain cloud had squeezed its way into the kitchen. I can't bear it when Mom cries. The world looks as dark as if God has switched off the light.

I should probably have noticed much earlier that some-thing wasn't right, because even her Japanese robe hung off her sadly. Instead of thinking about Mom, I had been busy with my own problems. When I saw her crying, I was sorry I'd thought up the burst-pipe story. Somebody not showing up and a canceled bingo evening are not as bad as a dying brother, even if you can't stand him. Mom's unhappiness was bigger than mine.

I got up, went around the table, and put my arms around her. Mom buried her face in my shoulder. Her hair smelled of a mixture of shampoo and the nightclub. She held me so tight I could barely breathe. That's how Molly One must have felt right before the *crack*

Just when I thought I couldn't take it any longer, she let go of me. She drew the back of her hand across her eyes. "I'll make it up to you, love, I promise," she sniffed. "But right now—"

"It's OK."

"You'll have to take care of yourself for a few days. You'll manage, won't you? You're a big boy."

"Of course."

"I'll leave you some money, and if you need anything, you go and see Mrs. Darling, all right? I'll leave her a note and try to call her at the supermarket."

"Don't worry. I'll go and see her this evening and tell her myself."

"I just want to make sure you're safe, Rico. Remember you can call me anytime on my cell phone." She took hold of me by the shoulders, pushed me a little distance away from her, and looked into my eyes. "I love you more than anything! You know that, don't you?"

I really wanted to say I was sorry and tell her I hadn't meant to say what I said, but suddenly I was all mixed up. I'd just thought of something terrible and not even the lottery balls in my head were working right. They clacked together for a moment or two, then fell still, as though they were frozen. The terrible thought was this: If Mom's brother had cancer, maybe she'd get it, too, because she —

"Rico?"

"Hmm?" Tears were running down my cheeks and snot was dribbling out of my nose and I didn't have a tissue.

"Cancer isn't catching. Do you hear me?"

I snorted something.

"You don't have to worry about that."

I snorted again, but I felt better. Mom never lies to me.

She raised one hand and wiped my face with the sleeve of her robe. She finally had a smile on her face, even if it was as faint as a snail's tracks.

"Christian phoned very early this morning," she explained. "Then I couldn't fall asleep, but I must have dozed off, and now it's late and the train leaves at two thirty. I wish I could do something about your little friend with the helmet, but I still have to pack, take a shower, get myself together, and buy a ticket at the station. . . ."

"Go ahead," I said.

I watched her as she stumbled out of the kitchen past her bedroom. The door was open. I could see her four-poster bed with the fancy shiny sheets and the posters of dolphins and whales on the walls.

I slowly calmed down. Mom wasn't getting cancer, we'd go to bingo next Tuesday, and Oscar would show up at some point. I remembered that he'd said he had something important to do today. Maybe that was more important than taking a walk by the canal and he would show up later. And even if he came tomorrow or the day after tomorrow, I still had something to look forward to: Mrs. Darling would definitely feed me whole wheat crackers this evening and we'd watch television together, even though it wasn't a weekend! If I could convince her to watch a Miss Marple movie, that was almost as good as playing bingo. I wouldn't be able to convince her to play bingo, though. Mrs. Darling thinks bingo is for old fogies who hitch their pants up under their armpits.

Life had just been shadowier than the shadowiest shadowy shadows. Now it was bright again. I felt bad for a minute that I didn't feel sorry for Uncle Christian, but he shouldn't have shouted the way he did when he'd argued with Mom. I had been so afraid that I'd hidden under the bed, and that's where I'd found Molly Two. She was all the way in the back in an old sneaker I'd grown out of. Maybe she'd been looking for other hamsters back there.

The sneaker stank.

Just after two o'clock Mom's taxi arrived. I went downstairs with her. The driver stashed her big suitcase in the trunk. Mom blew me a kiss from the backseat and then they drove off. I waved after her. I almost thought I could see the sad black rain cloud floating after the taxi.

I went upstairs and sat back down in the thinking chair for a while. I didn't know what I was going to do until the evening. I could water the KKs' flowers, but what if Oscar showed up just when I was upstairs on the fifth floor?

But Oscar wasn't going to show up.

It was my own fault. I should have asked him for his telephone number or at least what his last name was so that I could look it up in the phone book. I didn't really know anything about him, not even where he lived.

"It's your own fault," I repeated quietly.

Now I would have to spend the entire day by myself until I went to Mrs. Darling's in the evening.

I read a comic.

I drank orange juice.

I ran downstairs to the first floor and rang Bert's bell.

Bert is a lot of fun, but he wasn't at home. Just my luck. And if Oscar had showed up in the meantime and rung the bell, double bad luck, but then I could at least drop in on old Mr. Mommsen the superintendent on the ground floor. He tells exciting stories sometimes, like the one where Miss Friedmann exploded, and he always has some chocolate in the cupboard. But mostly he's just drunk and it's the booze talking.

BOOZE: Everything that makes you drunk. Alcohol. Usually the cheaper stuff. After drinking it most people come up with nonsense, which is what is meant by "it's the booze talking." I didn't have to look that up. You can figure some things out all by yourself.

Mr. Mommsen is a widower and fat and he doesn't have nice teeth. He probably doesn't brush them very much. Julie once said he was an old goat and no woman would be interested in him, so he probably has gray days, too. If today was one of his gray days and if it spread to Mrs. Darling's apartment, I wasn't sure I could cope. After Mom's rain cloud and my own elephant feeling, I'd had enough sadness for one day.

So I went back upstairs.

There was nothing happening on the stairs. It was so quiet in the building that it was almost a bit creepy. Normally there's noise coming from somewhere: Bert and Julie and Massoud have their music turned up, or the Kessler twins are screaming at each other, or there's some classical *tra-la-la* from Mr. Kirk's apartment. You can even hear noise coming from the very top floor when the KKs' chubby son, Freddy, brings his friends home and plays PlayStation with them with the volume turned up. Mr. Fitz has complained a hundred times, but it doesn't stop them.

Today there was zilch. Absolute quiet.

I went back into the apartment.

I turned the TV on and five minutes later I turned it off.

I put my dirty laundry in the washing machine.

I made my bed.

I sat on my bed.

Boring.

There was no point waiting. Oscar wasn't coming. And if he did come, he could go and jump in the canal. I wasn't going to let the KKs' flowers die of thirst just because of him.

So up I went.

By the time I got to the top, I wasn't angry at Oscar anymore. It wasn't his fault that I was bored. It wasn't his fault that our walk along the canal filled up my head like a balloon and that there wasn't any room for anything else.

Most of the KKs' plants were still wet enough. I watered the rest.

Then I went back downstairs.

I bumped into Mr. Marrak between the third and second

floors. He was wearing his fancy red work clothes and carrying his laundry bag, which was full to bursting. The first time Mrs. Darling saw him struggling with it, she put both hands to her head. "Typical man!" she said. "He waits until he's down to his last pair of underpants and his last shirt and then his girlfriend's supposed to stay up all night just so he has something to wear!" Nobody has ever seen his girlfriend at 93 Dieffe Street, but clearly Mr. Marrak doesn't have a washing machine.

"Hello, Mr. Marrak," I said, and tried to get past him.

"Hi, Rico." He put his laundry bag down with some effort and nodded at me. "Are you wandering around again? Whose apartment are you nosing in today?"

He didn't mean it nastily. When I went to look at his apartment after we moved in, he even offered me a Coke. Of course by then Mom had already told him I was a child proddity and that I liked to look at other people's apartments because I could only keep going straight on the street and didn't get to see much of the world. Mom had told everybody in the building and, except for Mr. Fitz, all the neighbors were very kind and let me in when I knocked on their door. Some of them let me in a few times, like Mrs. Darling or Bert, Julie, and Massoud. The Kesslers have asked a couple of times if I want to drop by again, but their twins get on my nerves.

Last time I went to Mr. Marrak's he even gave me his business card, the one with the golden safe on it. Now when we bump into each other we're very polite, but he's never invited me into his apartment again. I always hope that one day he'll open the little white house on the roof terrace with one of his many keys, but it doesn't seem likely. Grown-ups are always worrying about doing things that are illegal.

ILLEGAL: When you're not allowed to do something because it's forbidden and the police might not like it. LEGAL means it's allowed (and OOPS means that you've done something you're not allowed to and are hoping nobody will notice).

"I was watering the Kaminsky-Kowalskys' flowers," I explained to Mr. Marrak. "They're on vacation."

"Who?"

"What?"

"The flowers or the Kaminsky-Kowalskys?"

I looked at him, puzzled. Was he winding me up? Since when do houseplants go on vacation?

He was grinning. "Just teasing. A Rico tease. Don't you get it?"

He must have a screw loose!

"Didn't even notice that my charming neighbors had taken off," he added as though nothing had happened.

I would have liked to tell him he wasn't likely to notice anything when he spent all day running here, there, and everywhere with his jangling bunch of keys, carrying his stinky underwear around in a huge laundry bag. What an idiot!

"Don't look so angry!" He thumped my arm. "It was just a joke. A little bit of ribbing from one man to another. I didn't mean to upset you. Sorry, OK?"

"OK," I said slowly.

I don't like having my leg pulled. But in this case I made an exception and I decided to be only a little bit angry because Mr. Marrak is usually friendly to me. But that was as far as I would go. He's big and tall and has a chunky face, but otherwise there's nothing unusual about him. He isn't a good choice for Mom. He already has a girlfriend, after all, and it wouldn't be much fun washing his clothes while he went out with another woman. And then there'd be cleaning and tidying up and everything. Mr. Marrak is very messy. When I visited his apartment it looked like a bomb had hit it. If he wasn't careful, he'd let himself go and end up like Mr. Fitz, stinking in front of the cheese counter at the supermarket.

"OK, moving on, then!" He bent down to pick up the bag of laundry. "Say hello to your mom from me."

"I can't; she's gone away for a few days."

He stopped what he was doing, stood up straight again, and looked at me. "And who's keeping an eye on you till she gets back?"

"Me and Mrs. Darling."

"I see." His bottom lip was sticking out as if he didn't like what he'd heard. "To be perfectly honest, I don't understand some parents. They bring children into the world and then leave them to their own devices all day, either in front of the TV or the computer—"

"I don't spend all day sitting in front of—"

"Or they let their little ones romp around alone. If you ask me, Mr. 2000 should be a lesson to them all!"

"My mother doesn't leave me—"

"If those children who were kidnapped hadn't been running around alone in the big city, nobody would have been able to snatch them! That's just my opinion, of course!"

Now I was angry again, but instead of answering back, I just nodded. I should have stuck up for Mom, but Mr. Marrak wasn't listening to me, anyway. His pale face had gone all pink and looked like one of Mom's bath sponges. If I said anything, he would just keep on complaining, and when he'd finally gotten it all out of his system, he might ask me to help him carry his bag.

"I've got to go," I said.

"Me too," he said, finally balancing the huge bag of laundry on his shoulder. "Take care."

"Yup."

I jumped down the final steps to the second floor. As I let myself into the apartment, I could hear Mr. Marrak huffing and puffing his way up the stairs. "Stupid fifth floor," he grumbled. "Next time I'm moving in somewhere with an elevator!"

It's his own fault, I thought. He should buy himself a washing machine!

I'd only been back in the apartment a few seconds when the boredom picked up where it had left off.

I sat in the thinking chair.

I flicked through the dictionary and learned three new words.

I looked out the window and snoozed.

I forgot the three new words.

I went into the kitchen and drank some more juice.

I ate some more Crunchy Nut Clusters.

I washed the glass and the cereal bowl and the spoon.

My eyes fell on the trash can. The bag was full to the brim—something to do! If I took the garbage out to the yard and then wrote in my diary, the afternoon would go much faster.

So I went back downstairs again.

The giant trash cans are in the backyard, along the wall we share with the building next door. You have to pull pretty hard on one half of the large double doors that lead into the yard, because it's been sticking for a few weeks. The other half doesn't open at all. Mr. Mommsen, the superintendent, should have fixed it a long time ago because it's just getting worse, but he's too busy boozing. Even the garbage men have complained about it.

I tugged the sticking door until I could just about fit through with my bag of garbage, and I crashed straight into Mr. Mommsen. He was armed with a large broom and a small dustpan. I remembered that Tuesday was his day to sweep the yard.

"Hello, Mr. Mommsen," I said.

He staggered a little and stared at me. "Who are you?"

"Rico Doretti. Second floor."

"I know that," he said. "Do you think I'm stupid or something?"

Can you believe it?

Instead of answering, I held the door open for him as wide as I could manage. He pushed past me and looked me right in the face. His eyes looked milky.

"The door needs to be fixed," I said.

"Go and play!" he snapped.

"I will. See you later!"

"I hope not."

The door clicked shut in slow motion. I shook my head and went over to the trash cans. I pushed up the heavy black lid and threw in the bag of garbage, and then I saw it. In the middle of the dirty, stinky mess, a small, bright red airplane.

I looked up at the sky, as I had done when I had found the string of spaghetti. Dark clouds were forming and pushing themselves in front of the sun. Right up at the top, on the KKs' roof terrace, a final ray of sun glinted on the metal railing. I looked down again. There was only one way that the little airplane could have landed down here: It must have come loose from Oscar's shirt when he was standing up there yesterday, showing me he wasn't afraid. The airplane must have spun down into the yard and somebody must have picked it up and thrown it away. It had probably been drunken Mr. Mommsen, just a few minutes ago.

I stood on my tiptoes and tried to fish the airplane out of the trash can without getting dirty. It took a while, but finally I reached it. There was no dirt on it. I tapped the broken-off wing, then I put it into my jeans pocket and grinned. Oscar would be really happy when I gave him back his badge! He was probably missing it already.

Then I went back up to the second floor where my diary was waiting for me. Now I'm looking forward to a nice evening with Mrs. Darling and whole wheat crackers! Which means I have to go back *up* and then back *down* again.

Flippin' heck!

ALMOST
WEDNESDAY
the special edition

About ten minutes ago both of Mickey Mouse's arms showed twelve. So it's already after midnight.

In the backyard an enormous shadowier shadow has just moved, I'm sure of it. That's why I've moved from my room into the living room, into the thinking chair.

All the lights are on, but even if they were off you still couldn't see the moon through the window. It's darkest night outside. A stormy wind is moving the branches of the trees, rustling their leaves and driving drizzly rain against the windowpanes.

I've brought my bedspread with me and covered my legs with it. I'm sitting in front of the computer, writing my diary. I have to write down what happened this evening right away, otherwise I won't be able to get to sleep. And I have to think up a plan.

If only I could think more quickly.

Mrs. Darling knows nothing.

If I call Mom, I'll just worry her.

It's up to me.

I'm really scared.

Just before seven thirty I went upstairs to Mrs. Darling's. I didn't want to miss the local evening news. Well, actually, I didn't want to miss the whole wheat crackers, but saying I didn't want to miss the evening news sounds less greedy.

Anyway, I rang Mrs. Darling's bell. No reply. I pressed my ear to the door and listened. Nothing. Then I remembered. Mrs. Darling and I almost always see each other on Saturdays, which is her day off. I'd completely forgotten that she works until eight during the week. She couldn't be home yet. At that very moment she was probably standing behind the meat counter, wrapping up the final pork chop. Sometimes I can be such an idiot!

On the floor above me somebody was crunching around on the stairs. Then I heard a cheerful little whistle. It couldn't be Mr. Fitz; he has to be the least cheerful person on the planet. A door closed. Then there was silence.

So I went up to the fourth floor. A heavy blue bag of garbage was sitting in the stairway. Strips of wallpaper and bits of plastic wrap splattered with red and yellow and orange were poking out. Great! Mr. Haven was at home, and I had half an hour to spare. If I went about it the right way, I was sure he would let me into his apartment.

When I rang, he opened the door immediately. He looked at me in astonishment. With concern, almost.

"Rico! Did something happen?"

Why do so many people ask if something has happened when a kid rings their doorbell?

I shook my head and stretched out a hand. "Good evening! My name is Frederico Doretti. I'm—"

"Ehm . . . I know who you are."

He wouldn't let me finish! Some people can't even keep quiet for ten seconds, and what I had to say was almost as difficult as the thing about Mr. Marrak's Alarms, Safes, and Locks business. Somewhere in my head a small switch flicked on almost by itself and started up the lottery machine. I was hot and uncomfortable. I dropped my hand. I'd have to forget about shaking his. You can't concentrate on everything at the same time, after all, and up until now Mom had always said this part for me.

"My name is Frederico Doretti!" I repeated in a loud voice. "I'm a child proddity! That's why I can only walk straight ahead and don't see much of the world!" I got faster and faster. "That's why I like looking at other people's apartments canicomeinplease?"

Suddenly I wanted to turn on my heels and run away. If you knew ten seconds before you said or did something how stupid you would feel ten seconds later, you probably wouldn't say or do a lot of what you do say and do. But it was too late now.

"Child proddity?" Mr. Haven's eyebrows had slid together in the middle.

"That means I can think a lot but not particularly quickly," I squeezed out a further sentence.

"Ohhh-kay," he said very slowly.

"But that doesn't mean I'm stupid. For example, the moon is two hundred and thirty-eight thousand, eight hundred and fifty-five miles away from the earth. On average."

"I see." Very slowly again.

"The day before yesterday I didn't know that and it's very likely I'll forget it again soon. Sometimes a few things go missing from my brain, but I don't know when and where until it happens."

"Well, if that's the way things are . . ." Mr. Haven was smiling now, and it was a nice smile. He pulled the door open toward him. "Come on in."

About time!

I pushed past him and he closed the door. The smell of paint hit my nose. There were boxes all the way down the hall, most of them piled up on top of other boxes, some of them closed, others open

"I hope you don't mind the mess," Mr. Haven said. "I'm still moving in."

I shook my head. The mess was perfectly OK as long as he could get used to things being tidy, just in case he married Mom.

The door next to me was open, so I went in. It was the

living room, and it looked like winter itself in there. Instead of a carpet there was a wooden floor, painted white. The walls were white and so were the shelves. The shelves were only half-full, with books and CDs standing and sitting on them. I couldn't see a picture or a poster anywhere; there were no nice knickknacks like in Mrs. Darling's or our apartment. There was a white leather sofa with a table in front of it. An empty glass was standing on an open newspaper. The bottom of the glass was wet and had made a wavy stain right across one page. Other than that there were all kinds of things scattered across the table: pens, a notebook, receipts, and so on. In one corner of the room a small TV was standing on the floor, and in the other corner there was a stereo system.

"Everything fine and dandy?" Mr. Haven said behind me.

It sounded like the kind of question you ask when you don't know what else to say. It also sounded like a question you can only answer with a yes, so I murmured yes.

DANDY: Somebody like Mr. Kirk from the third floor who's got a lot of clothes and spends a lot of time in front of the mirror. I washed my face and put on a clean T-shirt before leaving the apartment, so maybe that's what Mr. Haven meant.

I folded my hands behind my back and looked up at the ceiling. At least the ceiling was pretty—very pretty, in fact:

old-fashioned plaster, and the only part of the room that was painted in a color.

"How's your mom?"

The ceiling looked a bit like a rain forest. There were all kinds of flowers and leaves in orange and yellow and red wrapped up in each other. A few of them looked so real they could have been growing down from the ceiling. Mom would like it. . . .

"Rico?"

"Hmm?"

"Your mom."

"She thinks you're the hottest thing she's ever met in her life. But . . ."

A little green in between the other colors would have been nice. Or something completely different from all the flowery, leafy things. I wondered if you could get plaster shapes like fish. Then your ceiling would look like an aquarium. You could have a turtle coming out of one corner and a bright little fish out of the other. And in the middle a blue whale, as big as—

Mr. Haven cleared his throat loudly. I turned around in his direction. He was standing in the doorway with his thumbs stuck in his pants pockets. He was smiling again, but at the same time he looked impatient, like somebody who can't wait until his aquarium has been put together.

"Yes?" he said. "But?"

"Well, I guess she can't fall in love with you because then she'd have to think about Dad."

"Oh—I see." Now he wasn't smiling anymore. He looked at me as though he'd just got a bad grade on a test. "I, um, I thought you lived alone?"

"We do. Dad has been dead for a long time."

And now he was looking at me as though the teacher had just given him the wrong test back and he'd gotten ten out of ten after all. His face was very tan, as if he'd spent the last few days in the sun. The only pale part was the little scar on his chin.

"I'm very sorry for you." His voice was suddenly so warm, I had the feeling the whole wintry room around me was thawing. "I'm very sorry for both of you!"

"He died on a stormy day," my voice said all by itself. "It was in autumn. Dad wanted—"

There was a noise like a cell phone. It had a cool ringtone. It sounded like a mouse running over the keys of a piano.

"I'm sorry!" Mr. Haven lifted one finger. "Don't run away, OK? I've been waiting for this call. It won't take long." He turned around and ran out of the room. The noise stopped.

Frederico, I thought, *you must be crazy!* I had been about to tell Mr. Haven my biggest secret, and I wasn't even friends with him. How had he managed to make me do that? When he came back, I'd tell him I was sorry but I had to go.

He had disappeared into the room diagonally across from where I was. I stretched out my neck—it was the kitchen. He was speaking into his cell phone in a low voice. I didn't understand a word, and before I could creep into the hallway to hear better, the phone call was already over. I drew my head back and looked casual.

"I'm afraid I have to go," Mr. Haven said when he came back. He still looked nice, but he was acting all businesslike. He had a brown leather jacket in his hand. "But I've got a suggestion," he said as he slipped it on. "Why don't you come back tomorrow in the late afternoon? Then I'll have a bit more time for you. And for your story. Agreed?"

"I don't know if—"

"If you don't want to tell me after all, you don't have to. But the invitation stands, OK?" He pointed to the door and tried to smile, but couldn't hide his tension. "And now off with you, you nosy child proddity!"

Mrs. Darling beamed at me like Halley's Comet when she saw me standing in front of her door, and suddenly I realized that she had more gray days than she would like. For the first time I wondered why she didn't have any children of her own.

"Mom had to go away," I said as she let me in. "She won't be back until the day after tomorrow at the earliest."

"Yes, Rico, she called me to ask if I could look after you. Where's she gone again?"

"To see her brother at the bottom and left. He's got cancer."

"How terrible!" Mrs. Darling pushed the door shut and turned around with a look of shock on her face. "Where?"

"At the bottom and left."

"I know that. I meant which part of the body?"

"Oh . . . no idea."

Mrs. Darling shook her head sadly. "It's always the wrong person who gets it."

"Who'd be the right person, then?"

"That superintendent," she said without batting an eyelid.

"What's up with him?"

"I had words with him as I came in. The door to the backyard has been sticking for weeks, you've probably noticed." She was so annoyed she didn't even wait for me to nod. "You can barely get it open when you take the trash out; it's getting worse by the day! But do you think that walking bottle of whiskey has done anything about it?"

I shrugged my shoulders and followed her past the pictures of laughing clowns into the kitchen. "At least cancer isn't catching," I said to get her off the subject. If she kept on complaining, she might forget about the whole wheat crackers.

"Did you think it was?" she asked over her shoulder.

"Of course not! I just thought you might not know that."

Unlike stupid Mr. Marrak, Mrs. Darling obviously didn't think it was too bad that Mom had left me by myself. She didn't mention it, in any case, and instead she finally got to the food.

"I was just about to make myself something to eat. Have you eaten already?"

"Crunchy Nut Clusters, this afternoon."

"Good, then we'll have some whole wheat crackers."

About time!

She opened the fridge to get the ham and cheese, pickled onions, and tomatoes. "By the way, it just so happens that I've bought a new movie."

I leaned against the table. "Is it a thriller?"

"A romance. *While You Were Sleeping.*"

She took some bread out of the cupboard. "Now, let me make the food. Have a seat in the living room and turn on the boob tube. Then you can tell me what's going on in the world while we're eating."

She was talking about the news. I would rather have just kept watching her.

"I won't remember."

"Yes, you will. You've got an amazing memory; don't let anybody tell you any different."

She waggled the bread knife in front of my nose. "Off you go, shoo, shoo! I don't like people getting under my feet in the kitchen."

I went into the living room grumpily. I flopped onto the sofa, grabbed the remote control, and switched on the giant TV. It's always set to the local channel so that Mrs. Darling never misses her beloved newscaster. Before the picture came on, a woman's voice could be heard.

"—*who has been terrorizing Berlin for three months, has, it has just been announced, kidnapped his sixth victim. Our special edition will fill you in on the latest developments—in a case that is surprisingly different from its predecessors.*"

You could see the woman reporter now; she was one of Peter Duffel's colleagues. Now and then they took turns doing the news from Berlin. The woman was trying to look concerned because there was a child involved. I didn't believe her, though. Grown-ups always look concerned on television when there's a child involved in a crime, and then in the supermarket they shove their shopping carts into your back or almost push you into the freezer compartment if you get in their way.

But it was exciting all the same. The newscaster explained that it was unusual for the kidnapper to have released a child just last Saturday only to have snatched another one straightaway. She was right. It was pretty quick. Maybe Mr. 2000 had been afraid he wouldn't be able to get any kids over the summer because everybody would be away on vacation.

A map of Berlin came up on the screen, and they highlighted all the different parts of the city, one after another.

"There appears to be no pattern to the kidnappings. The police are assuming that Mr. 2000 drives around aimlessly, luring children into his vehicle when a suitable opportunity presents itself."

Next up on the screen was Schöneberg, where Mom and I live. It had to be where the latest victim was from. The other parts of town weren't shown, but six red dots flashed on the map to show where the kidnappings had been.

"Well?" Mrs. Darling called out from the kitchen. "Any news?"

"The ALDI kidnapper has snatched another kid!"

"Gracious me. Turn it up! Milk or juice?"

"Milk, please!"

I turned the volume up with the remote.

"For the first time in this series of kidnappings, the father of the victim has turned to the police without paying the ransom money demanded."

The six parts of town and the red dots turned into shaky camera shots. The upper right corner of the screen said LIVE. A youngish man who looked kind of scruffy came into view. There were so many microphones being held in front of his nose that you could barely see his face in the crush. He kept blinking, because the flash of the cameras dazzled him. Reporters were calling out questions all around him.

"Why did you notify the police? The kidnapper usually threatens the kidnapped children with—"

"I don't have the money," said the man. "It's as simple as that." And he added with a snort, "I had to go to the police because no bank in the world would have given me a loan. Not even for a kidnapped child."

"What's a loan?" I called out to the kitchen.

"Money that you borrow from somebody for a while," Mrs. Darling called back. "But in the end you have to pay more back than you borrowed in the first place."

I was just about to ask her if she wanted to borrow some money from me, but at that very moment the television showed a photo of the latest victim and my heart almost stopped.

The child was a boy.

The boy was Oscar.

He wasn't wearing his helmet, but I recognized him right away. Nobody has green eyes like Oscar and nobody has teeth that big. It could very well be that nobody has sticky-out ears like that, either. They stood out almost horizontally from Oscar's head. You could easily put a small glass containing a cold drink on each one.

"As the father of the boy explained, his seven-year-old son left home at around nine o'clock to visit a friend. But little Oscar never arrived."

I barely understood what the newscaster was saying. There was a strange buzzing in my ears. Now Oscar's dad was surrounded by reporters again.

"I don't know why he went out without his helmet. Normally he never leaves the house without his helmet! We live in a big city. Our streets are dangerous. I was always telling him that."

"Why didn't you accompany your son? Wasn't that neglecting your parental duty?"

"No comment."

"Did you know *who* Oscar was going to visit? Are you sure that the friend he was going to visit actually exists?"

"No comment."

"At ten thirty this morning, Oscar's father, who is a single parent, received a call from the kidnapper. That, too, is unusual: Up until now the kidnapper has always contacted the parents of his victims by letter. The kidnapper's demand, however, is the same as

always: two thousand euros. A meeting place for the handover of the ransom money has not yet been agreed upon."

The buzzing in my ears grew less. *Two thousand euros,* I thought, *two thousand euros.* Oscar's father obviously didn't have any rich friends or relatives who could lend him that much money. He didn't have a wife, either. And Oscar almost certainly did not have a piggy bank. For somebody who was so afraid, that really wasn't very sensible. Even I had started saving up for my own kidnapping.

I jumped when Mrs. Darling showed up like a ghost and put the plate with the whole wheat crackers down on the table. I hadn't heard her coming into the living room. She plumped up the soft cushion with the tassels that she always puts behind her back and sat down next to me on the sofa.

"Maybe they'll catch the swine now!" she snorted. "Maybe somebody saw the boy this morning and will remember."

She leaned back on the cushion, stuck a cracker into her mouth, and chewed it. Boiled ham with a pickled onion. I looked at her secretly from the side. She would probably believe me if I said that I not only knew Oscar but that he'd been on the way to see me this morning. And because she'd believe me, she'd drag me to the police so they could question me. Where did I know Oscar from and how long had I known him and when had we last seen each other and at what point had we arranged to meet and at what time? What had we talked about? Had Oscar mentioned anything that would suggest he knew his kidnapper? The police would take me apart the way Miss Marple treated her suspects. The lottery machine would go crazy.

I'd die of embarrassment.

On the TV they were now showing the picture of the first kidnapped child. I knew what was coming next; they'd done it a thousand times already: They'd show one kid after another. Sad music was playing, as though the victims had all been through a shredder instead of coming back in one piece.

"Now they're just trying to make us cry," said Mrs. Darling. "I'd better put the movie on. What did I do with it? Oh yes, I think it's in my handbag."

She pushed herself up from the sofa and disappeared into the hall. I just kept staring at the screen, dazed. My friend Oscar was the latest kidnap victim and he didn't even have a mom to worry about him! She was probably dead or something like that. I couldn't believe it. I should have been afraid for Oscar or felt sorry for him, but as the pictures of the kidnapped children were being shown, I felt like a bowl that had been completely licked clean of cake mix.

When the second victim popped up, I looked more closely. They'd gotten a new photo of Sophia. Her parents finally seemed to have realized that the TV kept showing the same terrible picture of their daughter, and had given the evening news a better one. Sophia was standing in a playground next to a rocking horse on springs. The photo must have been taken in the playground in front of her grade school, because in the background you could see a big building with colorful pictures stuck to the windows, probably from the inside.

Unlike the old blurry photo, this one was really clear. Sophia didn't look much prettier in it than she usually did, but she did look much nicer. She was smiling. Her hair was washed and she was no longer wearing the wrinkled pink T-shirt with the big fat strawberry jam stain on the chest, but an ironed light blue one instead. However . . .

I leaned forward. It was hard to believe, but Sophia had stained her light blue T-shirt in almost exactly the same place! The camera zoomed in on the picture. And for the second time that evening my heart stood still. It wasn't a stain, I could see that now.

It was a small, bright red airplane with a broken-off wing.

WEDNESDAY
looking for sophia

Dear Mom,

I have left the computer on on purpose so that you'll find my diary right away when you come home. I don't want you to worry, but I have to help Oscar. The boy with the blue helmet. If something happens to me, you can break into my piggy bank to pay for the funeral. If Uncle Christian has died, you can put me in his coffin. If I'm dead, I won't mind.

Love,
Rico

P.S. Mr. Haven will take care of you. He's very nice and has a beautiful living room, especially the ceiling. I love you!

It was eight thirty in the morning and the day was fresh and wet. I stood in front of 93 Dieffe Street and looked into a dirty puddle that the rain had left behind on the pavement the night before. Seeds from the trees with the peeling-off bark were raining into the puddle, hundreds and hundreds of them. They looked like tiny parachutists.

I was well equipped. Mom's *A to Z* map of Berlin was in my backpack. I had the money that she'd left me, too—twenty euros. And when I patted the front pocket of my jeans, I could feel the red airplane that I had fished out of the trash can.

One thing was clear: Sophia must have given Oscar the airplane as a present—this very airplane with the broken-off wing. I couldn't imagine that he'd stolen it.

But why had he visited Sophia?

What had she told him?

Though on the one hand it was sort of difficult to believe, on the other I couldn't help suspecting that Oscar had tried to track down Mr. 2000 all by himself. I didn't know where he had got hold of that crazy idea and why his search had brought him to Dieffe Street last Saturday. But he must have been following a clue that he had gotten from Sophia. A really important clue that Sophia had either not told the police or that nobody had believed when she had told them.

My head was spinning so much it hurt. Maybe Mr. 2000 hadn't chosen Oscar, but had kidnapped him because Oscar had been on his trail. Had Oscar been planning to catch Mr. 2000 by offering himself up as bait? And if that was the case, why hadn't Oscar let anybody in on his plan?

The thoughts were flying wildly around my head, like chickens squawking because they're being chased by somebody with a meat cleaver. The night before, I had fallen asleep in the thinking chair from all the effort, but before I did I had the idea of looking for Sophia. Now here I was, trying to set out to find Sophia but rooted to the spot, staring at this stupid puddle.

Oh God, oh God!

I'd never been out of my street by myself. I'd been with other people, though. Irina has a fast car, and on nice summer days Mom and I go for drives with her. We cruise from Alexander Square to the radio tower and back, past the Brandenburg Gate and then into the center of the city, listening to cool music. If we like the look of a street, then we get out and sit at a trendy sidewalk cafe. The sun shines on Irina's golden ankle chain and on Mom's fingernails with their pink shimmer or whatever else is on them, and Mom and Irina drink champagne and laugh themselves silly, and I drink Coke and I'm happy that so many people think Mom is great. Everybody looks at her, but Mom never asks any of them if they'd like some of her champagne.

But getting around Berlin by myself is another matter. The very idea of setting off to find Sophia without really knowing which way to go froze me to the sidewalk. I wasn't brave enough to open Mom's large *A to Z* of the city. All those lines and bright colors and then the tiny letters and all those funny symbols. Not for Rico!

What a great start.

I turned around as the door to the building opened behind

me. Mr. Kirk isn't as good-looking as Mr. Haven, but he's not much worse-looking. Mrs. Darling says he's always neat as a pin, and she's right. He wears extremely cool clothes and shoes and he has a huge collection of sunglasses. Mrs. Darling is always asking herself how he pays for all that stuff on his salary. Mr. Kirk also goes to the hairdresser's once a week, and he owns the coolest car on all Dieffe Street, an old Porsche where you have to wind the windows down by hand. The car was right on the other side of the street. Mr. Kirk had the key in his hand as he came out of the door.

Sometimes, when you have a good idea, it's almost as though you can't breathe for a moment. Unfortunately everybody notices because of the color of your face. Mr. Kirk could see it even through his dark glasses.

"Everything all right, Rico?" he said.

I forced myself to breathe in and nodded. We don't know each other that well. Mr. Kirk hadn't been all that impressed when I wanted to look at his apartment, and when we meet in the stairway, we almost never talk.

"You're up early," he said. "Aren't you on summer break?"

"I was waiting for you," I said.

He pushed up his sunglasses in surprise. "For me?"

"I'm going in your direction," I said. The dental laboratory where he works is in the part of town where Sophia lives, Tempelhof. I should have realized that a lot earlier.

"Tempelhof? What are you up to over there?"

"Visiting a girl."

"Oh yeah?" He always looks like a bit of a show-off when he grins. "I thought nights were for visiting girls."

"Not a going-out-with kind of girl!" I said, though it's really none of his business. "So will you take me with you?"

"Be my guest!" he said, and pointed to the Porsche. "But if you get the car dirty, I'll throw you out right then and there!"

We crossed the street and he opened the passenger door for me. As soon as I was sitting in the car, I dug the *A to Z* out of my backpack, opened it, and ran my finger over it. Mr. Kirk got in on the other side, put his seat belt on, and glanced at the map.

"What are you looking for?"

"The school."

"Which school?"

"The one where I'm going to meet my friend on the playground."

"I thought you wanted to go to Tempelhof. Why are you looking at a page with a forest on it?"

It was one of the few double pages in the *A to Z* that didn't have many roads marked. Everything was nice and green because of all the trees, although up until a minute ago I'd thought they were fields. Most of the paths that were drawn in had very simple names, and the Havel River was flowing on one side, nice and blue. I stuck the *A to Z* under Mr. Kirk's nose.

"Could you look for me? I'm a bit lost," I admitted reluctantly.

"Because of your learning difficulties or what?"

I had to bite my lip to stay calm. The way he said it just like that, and the grin on his face! If I shouted at Mr. Kirk now, he'd never take me with him. It's annoying when people think you're totally stupid just because your brain works in a different way from theirs.

"I'm not a child proddity on purpose, and anyway I'm only a little bit of one," I said angrily, and pointed at the *A to Z.* "Sometimes I just don't know where front and back is and things like that."

"Really?" said Mr. Kirk. "Well, welcome to the club."

"It's nothing to be ashamed of."

"I never said it was."

"And I've got a really good memory."

"All right, all right!" He put both his hands up in the air as though I was threatening him with a pistol. "I'm sorry if I offended you. So, what's the name of the school?"

I leaned back in my seat. "I've forgotten."

He sighed impatiently. "Listen, kid, we won't get anywhere like this. There are God knows how many grade schools in Tempelhof; I can't possibly drive past all of them."

I wrinkled my nose. Mr. Kirk rolled his eyes.

"All right, then, listen. There's a school I drive past on my way to work. I'll drop you off there. After that you'll have to figure it out by yourself. I can't be late for work because of you."

I opened my mouth to reply.

"No ifs, ands, or buts!" He put his key in the ignition and mumbled so I could hardly understand, "I had enough problems on Monday for taking the afternoon off."

"What for?" I asked, interested. Monday was the day I'd seen him in the stairway with Mr. Haven and Mr. Marrak.

"That's of no interest to little boys."

"Why not?"

"Because it's got something to do with big boys."

I pushed myself even lower into my seat. "Are we going, then?"

"As soon as you've put your seat belt on, boss." Mr. Kirk pulled his sunglasses back over his eyes and turned the key. "And if you promise me that you'll keep your mouth shut while we're driving."

I was very lucky that the school where Mr. Kirk let me out turned out to be the right one. Who knows what would have happened otherwise? I recognized the building right away from the new picture of Sophia on TV—the red bricks, the decorated windows; I even discovered the rocking horse on springs in the playground.

Behind me Mr. Kirk drove off with screeching tires. I watched him go. Riding in the Porsche was awesome! It didn't feel like driving; it felt like floating over the ground. The motor had purred like a happy cat, and Mr. Kirk had barely needed to turn the steering wheel. True, that was because we had driven straight ahead for quite a while in the beginning, had only turned off once at a crossroads, and then driven straight ahead again for ages. But it had been cool. Mr. Kirk had put his foot on the accelerator impatiently at every traffic light. The engine had revved up and everybody had looked at us. It was great!

It was only the last part that was difficult: a little turn here and a little turn there, more crossroads, more traffic lights, and in between, the lottery balls in my head banging into each other and saying the same thing over and over again: *You'll never find the way home, you'll never find the way home.* . . .

We'd see about that!

I looked around. The playground in front of the school was empty. Almost nobody goes to a playground at nine thirty in the morning in the middle of summer. I was expecting that, but I knew that the longer I stayed here, the more chance I had of meeting somebody who could help me—a kid who went to school here, too, and knew Sophia, the famous girl who had been kidnapped.

I stomped around a bit. The seats on the swings glistened with water. The sand in the sandbox was dark gray and sticky. Fat drops of rain clung to the metal of the monkey bars. Off to one side, on the way to the school building, there was a bench. Two boys were sitting on the back of it. One of them had blond, stubbly hair and was about as tall as Oscar. The other one had untidy brown hair, was a lot bigger than I was, and was talking to stubblehead. If he was used to younger kids, he probably wouldn't tell me to get lost if he didn't like the look of me.

I wandered over to the two of them. The big one was so busy talking that he didn't notice me until I was only five feet away. The little one had been watching me the whole time without moving an inch.

"What?" said the big one as I stood in front of them. He didn't look mean or unfriendly, just annoyed at being disturbed.

"Do you know your way around here?" I asked him.

"Why?"

"I'm looking for someone who lives nearby."

I was only guessing, but most kids don't live far away from their school. Sophia might be only a few streets away in her room, organizing her T-shirts.

The big one didn't answer.

"Her name's Sophia and she goes to this school," I went on. "I don't know her last name. She's the girl who was abducted by the ALDI kidnapper."

He nodded as though people asked him about Sophia every day. "And if I do know where she lives?"

"You can tell me."

"What's your name?"

"My name's Rico."

"Felix."

"No, Rico." Hadn't he heard me?

"I'm Felix. So, what do you want from Sophia?"

"She's my friend."

"You don't know her last name and you don't know where she lives?" He laughed quietly. "You can't be friends."

"I can't remember addresses and things like that. I'm a child proddity."

Felix scrunched his eyebrows together. He didn't understand the word. It only took a second for me to battle with myself and say that other thing I hated: "I have learning difficulties. But only sometimes," I added quickly.

The blond stubblehead kept on looking at me without making a sound. He probably wasn't even breathing. He had light blue, somehow watery eyes that looked as though ladybugs could take a bath in them. I found him a bit freaky.

"So, assuming you *are* nice, just a bit weird," said Felix, "why should I tell you anything about Sophia?"

"Do you know where she lives, then?"

"I'm in the same class as Michael. He's a complete idiot." He thought for a second. "Maybe anyone would turn into a complete idiot if they had to share a room with their little sister. I know I'd go crazy."

"Who's Michael?"

"Sophia's brother, you brainwarp!"

That was it! First Mr. Kirk and now Felix, too. For the second time that morning I had to swallow my anger to continue. If I ever saw Oscar again, he owed me more than just a walk by the canal followed by an ice-cream cone. A lot more.

"If you'd been here five minutes earlier, you'd have bumped into Michael. His mom sent him shopping." He giggled quietly and pointed with one hand over his shoulder. "Over to ALDI."

"I just want to ask Sophia something," I said.

"What?"

He wouldn't take me to her unless I told him. He didn't say so, but I could see it on his face.

I took a deep breath. "The boy who was kidnapped yesterday . . ."

"What about him?"

"Sophia knows him. And I thought I'd ask her—"

"If she put him on the trail of Mr. 2000? You're crazy!" He let out a loud laugh. Then he turned serious again. "What do you think she can tell you? Stuff that she didn't already tell the police?"

"Something like that," I murmured.

"Because she'd rather trust a kid than a grown-up?"

I nodded. That had been my idea, and Oscar must have had the same one.

"Well, in that case . . ."

Felix suddenly swung himself off the bench. Stubblehead did the same thing.

"You know what you're getting yourself into, don't you?" said Felix as we left the playground. "Mr. 2000 himself, the most cunning kidnapper of all time! If he catches you, the first thing he'll do is cut your ears off."

"Says who?"

"Says me. They always cut your ears off first."

I hadn't known that.

"Then a hand! And then, if he still hasn't got his money, the arm it belongs to. He has to leave the other arm on so that you can still write your parents a begging letter, see? That's why he'll take your legs off next."

"You're making it up."

He shook his head and his brown hair got even more untidy. "Anyway, I want to write books one day, and writers make things up all the time, you know?"

"I only read comics."

"Well, they're completely made up."

It was difficult to keep up with him. He took huge steps. "And have you written anything yet?"

"A lot, actually."

"Is it good?"

"You'll have to ask Sam."

"Who's Sam?"

"Who do you think?"

Stubblehead still didn't say a word. He had to take twice as many steps as Felix to keep up, but he trotted along next to him as though he was fastened to him by an invisible rope.

"I tell him all my new ideas," said Felix. "If he thinks a story's good, I write it down. And not before."

I raised a hand and waved at Sam. "Hello, Sam."

No reply. Sam didn't even look at me.

"He can't hear you," said Felix. "He can't speak, either. He's deaf and dumb."

"You don't say 'deaf and dumb.' It's called 'hearing impaired.'" I knew that from school.

"Whatever." Felix walked even more quickly, looking straight ahead. "He's the only person who listens to me."

The apartment where Sophia lived was in between a lot of other apartments that all looked the same. They had no balconies, smooth front walls, and were painted brown. The wooden window frames looked as though they'd been white once.

Felix showed me which bell to ring before leaving for who knows where with Sam in tow. I watched the two of them go. How crazy do you have to be to tell your stories to somebody who's deaf? And how crazy do you have to be to listen to somebody you can't hear? Maybe they both knew sign language. Felix and Sam didn't seem embarrassed. They were friends. For them it was the most normal thing in the world. And that made me feel a lot better.

But not for long.

When Sophia's mom opened the door, a wave of gray day washed over me. There was even a gray smell. Sophia's mom didn't look like a mom who was interested in which children were in her kid's class at school. Luckily for me. She was wearing a grubby bathrobe and waved me into the apartment even before I'd finished saying my lines.

"Good morning. I'm a friend of Michael's and—"

"He's gone shopping."

I stood in front of her in a gloomy hallway. She pointed past my shoulder with one hand. In the other she was holding a smoking cigarette. "He'll be back soon. You can wait in his room."

I looked closely at her fingernails. They were splintered and painted pink. With no stickers. My mom would never go out in public with such scruffy nails. And she always combs her hair right after brushing her teeth.

Sophia's mom shuffled back into the living room. I could see a flat-screen TV through the open door. It was even bigger than Mrs. Darling's and had to be brand-new, because it was the only thing in the entire apartment that gleamed. I'd already been able to hear it clearly when I was outside the front door on the stairs. Here in the apartment, it was annoyingly loud. Two neighbors were arguing on a talk show. One of them had peed over the other one's garden fence and his neighbor's squash plant had died.

SQUASH: A game that you play with a racket and ball. No idea why anybody would pee on a squash racket or why you would plant one in the garden.

At the end of the hall there were two more rooms. On one of the doors there were colorful pictures and a Barbie poster. I knocked quietly and went in. If Sophia wasn't at home, I'd leave right away without telling anybody.

The room was the biggest mess I'd ever seen. Toys, clothes, comics, school stuff, CD covers, and computer games were scattered all over the floor. There were empty and half-empty bottles, used plates and cups lying all over the place. You would need days to clear a path through all that mess to get outside into the hall. And over everything lay a sad, gray cloud of dust. It was as if a vacuum-cleaner bag had exploded here fifty years ago.

Sophia was just standing there, in the middle of the room, as though she'd been waiting for someone for a long time or was practicing for a competition in falling asleep while on your feet.

"Hi!" I said.

Her thin, colorless eyebrows made a frown. Her gaze was cloudy, as though her eyes were trying not to be noticed in this gray room. Behind her a bunk bed stuck up out of the clutter like an island. She must get quite tired fighting her way into bed each night. I pulled the red airplane out of my pocket. Suddenly Sophia's eyes lit up.

"I got it from Oscar, and he got it from you," I said quickly. I didn't have a lot of time. Michael could come back from his shopping trip at any moment and tell his mom he'd never seen me before in his life.

She stared at the airplane. Her eyes filled with tears.

"He's in great danger—you know that, don't you?" I asked.

For a moment I was afraid she hadn't heard about Oscar's kidnapping, but then she nodded. I would have been surprised if she hadn't; the TV seemed to be on here all day. You could hear the bickering of the angry neighbors on the talk show even in here.

"You told Oscar something, didn't you?" I said carefully. "Something that you didn't tell the police because the kidnapper told you something terrible would happen if you did. Am I right?"

Finally she opened her mouth. Her voice was squeaky, like a bird that's just left the nest but doesn't trust itself to fly.

"The jingle-jangle man said if I tell on him, he'll come and get Marlon and kill him."

"Marlon?"

She pointed to a sticky desk that was so full you couldn't even have written a shopping list on it. There was a round goldfish bowl behind a greasy, crumpled McDonald's wrapper. Something was swimming around in it.

"That's Marlon. He's sick. He's got something on his fins."

Mr. 2000 must have asked Sophia who she loved best so that he could blackmail her into keeping quiet. And Sophia must have said her goldfish!

I stared at the round bowl and Marlon stared back. He

waggled two colorless, strangely frayed fins. I felt sick. Maybe the germs lurking between the piles of garbage were responsible for his illness. Maybe they were jumping germs. I breathed in very carefully and concentrated on Sophia again.

"Why do you call the kidnapper the jingle-jangle man?"

She shook her head slowly but stubbornly.

"You can tell me. I won't tell anybody."

"That's what Oscar said!" she said in an unexpectedly loud voice. "And now he's locked up in the green room!"

"Which green room?"

There was no reply.

"Sophia, Oscar is my friend," I insisted. "I want to help him, but I can't do that unless you help me!"

She glared at me suspiciously.

She clenched her little hands into fists.

Her narrow lips got even thinner.

There was nothing to be done. She wasn't going to tell me anything else. I held out the red airplane. She took it slowly, as though it was the most precious thing she'd ever been given. She stroked the broken wing with a clumsy finger.

"He said he liked me," she said quietly.

"He does. He wore the airplane all the time. But then he must have lost it. Maybe when he was kidnapped."

She looked up at me, very stubborn again. "I was expensive," she said.

"Yes, I know."

"But Mom got money for the interviews."

I nodded. That explained the new TV. The drone of it followed me out to the stairs as I left.

Now I had to get home. Back outside, things started to feel a little scary. The large buildings all around me seemed to be creeping closer together and bending down toward me. The dirty white windows stared at me like a thousand eyes. I rummaged around frantically in my backpack for the *A to Z*, opened it, looked inside, and closed it again immediately. I'll bet people have gone crazy trying to read the *A to Z*.

I'd have to go about it some other way. If I found a subway station, surely I'd manage. I just had to make it to the subway stop near my apartment on one of the lines; the rest would be easy. I can see the entrance to our subway station really well from the kebab restaurant whenever I'm eating there. From there to home it was just the other way around.

There was a shop on the other side of the street. I could ask the way there. There was no zebra crossing in sight, but there was hardly any traffic.

Every year almost forty thousand children in Germany die in accidents, I could hear Oscar saying. *Twenty-five percent are pedestrians.*

That must be more than a hundred, I guessed. I stretched one arm out just to be on the safe side, one hand pointing forward like an arrow, and ran straight across the street with my eyes shut tight.

No screeching of brakes, no honking. Everything went smoothly.

No accident.

In front of the shop there were all kinds of newspaper stands full of bold headlines about Oscar's kidnapping. In one newspaper there was a map similar to the one I'd seen yesterday on television, with six red dots on it showing the location of each kidnapping. Underneath it said: THE PATTERN OF TERROR! And in smaller letters: PARENTS' PANIC — COULD YOUR CHILD BE NEXT?

Either the woman at the counter hadn't read the newspapers or else she didn't care if kids ran around without their parents. Whichever it was, she didn't say anything about it when I asked her how to get to the nearest subway station.

I couldn't remember the directions she gave me. There was so much "turn left here" and "go right there" and "then left again" that I got really dizzy. But I said thank you in a friendly voice. It wasn't her fault that I could only walk in a straight line.

Back on the street I trudged along. There was bound to be a bus stop somewhere, or I might find the subway station.

Then I saw the line of taxis. I trotted up to them in relief. I had never taken a taxi in my life and I had no idea if Mom's twenty euros would get me all the way home, but it would be money well spent. At least Mom would get me back and wouldn't have to pick me up in the Alps or from the Pacific Ocean because I'd gotten lost.

I crawled into the backseat of the first car and closed the door behind me. The driver had a roll of fat at the back of his neck. He turned around to look at me.

"What are you doing?" he barked at me.

"What do you mean, what am I doing?"

"What's a garden gnome like you doing alone on the street? Where are your parents?"

I had pretty much had enough.

"I've got to go home, but I can't find the way," I said. "And before you ask why—I'm a child proddity!"

"Oh yeah? That's what all you brats are these days!"

I didn't want to talk back. I just wanted to be at home in the thinking chair. A jingle-jangle man and a green room . . . great! I didn't have the faintest idea what either of them meant. I had traveled all that way to see Sophia for nothing. Tears came to my eyes, but the taxi driver wasn't one bit sympathetic. He was still looking me up and down. I tried Oscar's trick and stared back at him, but it didn't work.

"I'll ask you again. Where are your parents?"

He wouldn't drive off until I'd given him some kind of answer that satisfied him. Honestly, how annoying! He knew his way around the city and didn't know what it felt like when you have problems with directions and your only friend has been kidnapped from under your nose.

"I was with a friend from school," I said finally. "My mom phoned. My dad is dead and I have to go home right away. She told me to take a taxi."

It was a pretty hopeless thing to say, but it worked. I finally started to cry and the taxi driver looked all worried. He turned around, started the car, and drove off. He didn't say another word until he'd dropped me off in front of my building on Dieffe Street, and when he took thirteen euros forty off me, he almost looked as though he felt bad about it.

WEDNESDAY AGAIN
shadowier shadows

Bad things take all your energy away and make your legs shake. By midday I had typed everything that had happened into my diary. Now I was sitting in the thinking chair, staring out the window and thinking about Felix telling his stories with no one to listen to them, about silent Sam with his ladybug-bath eyes, and about Sophia, surrounded by all those gray days. I thought about Oscar, locked up somewhere, very frightened even though he's so smart. Then I thought about me, sitting around here because I'm a child proddity and don't know what to do next. Somebody who is smarter than I am would have been able to get more clues out of Sophia.

DEPRESSION: Gray days. Mom called it that once when we were talking about Mrs. Darling. Depression is when all your feelings are in a wheelchair. They don't have arms anymore and sadly there's no one to push them, either. The tires are probably flat, too. It makes you very tired.

I crept into my room and lay down on the bed. Now and then I squinted through the window at the cracked front of the building behind ours, which looked less scary during the day than it did in the evening and at night when the shadowier shadows came. I could still be a little bit happy and proud, I thought, because I'd been brave enough to go to Tempelhof alone and had survived.

My eyes closed all by themselves. Last night I had slept badly and not for long enough. At one point I jumped out of bed because I thought the phone had rung, but the apartment was quiet. Then I dozed off again. I dreamt that Oscar was standing in front of me on the roof terrace. He had just proved his bravery by leaning over the railing and looking down into the backyard. Then he looked at me and I really wanted to know if he was my friend. I heard myself asking if he would come by again tomorrow. I saw Oscar scratching his arm. Fingering his airplane badge. Chewing on his lower lip with his large teeth before he said: *Actually, I've got plans for tomorrow. They could take all day.*

I woke up with a start, as though somebody had hit me in the head, only it didn't hurt. Something was wrong with the dream. Or something was wrong with my memory. I could almost reach it with both hands, but when I grasped for it . . .

Keep calm, Rico, don't get excited! I closed my eyes and called up the images again. Sun on the roof terrace. Oscar leaning against the railing that looks out on to the backyard, rock, rock, rocking. Scratching his arm. Fingering the airplane that I found the next day in the trash can, the small red airplane, the airplane —

—*that up until now I had thought had fallen off his shirt into the yard while he was swinging on the railing!*

I sat up in bed so fast that I got dizzy. My memory was wrong! Oscar had still been wearing Sophia's plane when he stepped back from the railing on the KKs' roof terrace. Which could only mean . . .

"He came back again later on," I whispered.

But when? After we said good-bye on Monday, I had seen Oscar from the living room window, leaving the building. I had fun counting the number of steps he took from the stairs down to the street, to find out if he was as fast as me. Oscar had been faster than my counting. On Monday he definitely hadn't been in the backyard, unless he'd come back later and had rung somebody else's doorbell—very unlikely. And on Tuesday, yesterday morning, he had already been kidnapped, probably while he was on his way to see me.

And that could only mean . . .

It could only mean . . .

I had no idea what it could, should, or had to mean. As always when I get worked up, I could feel my heart beating and a thousand birds fluttering through my head. I had to talk to somebody. Sometimes, when you tell people something that's got you really confused, you're less confused afterward.

And I knew exactly who I could talk to.

* * *

"I was wondering if you'd remember my invitation and stop by this afternoon," Mr. Haven said. "We agreed to meet, but . . ."

I hadn't forgotten. Most of all I remembered the warm feeling that flooded through me when I'd been about to tell him the story of my dead dad. How Mr. Haven looked at me and his wintry living room seemed to thaw around me. I felt like a little boat on top of high waves out in the open sea, and Mr. Haven was my port in the storm.

". . . but I had the impression you might have scared yourself with your own bravery."

"What's bravery?"

"It's when you are scared of something but you still face up to it."

I nodded. I'd learned a new word, but I had no idea how Mr. Haven had begun the sentence. If I admitted that to him, he'd probably think I was an idiot again, and it was important—at that moment it was the most important thing in the world—that Mr. Haven liked me. Mr. Haven had to help me find Oscar.

I sat in his white living room on his white sofa. I was careful not to look up at the beautiful plaster ceiling so I wouldn't get thinking about the aquarium and all that. There was a Coke on the table in front of me. I thought about asking Mr. Haven for whole wheat crackers, but he might have thought that was rude. He stood there with the cool scar on his chin, smiling that fantastic actor smile of his, looking down at me.

"Has your mom been in touch?" he said.

"I think she tried. The phone rang, but I was asleep."

I sipped my Coke carefully. You have to be careful with Coke. I've heard that if you drink too much of it, it burns holes in your stomach from the inside, and then the Coke glugs right up through you, and when you're at the cheese counter at the supermarket, you suddenly notice brown stuff running out of your nose.

"Don't you have a cell phone?" said Mr. Haven.

"Nah. Too expensive." To be honest, I wouldn't know who to call besides Mom.

You'd think Mr. Haven's cell phone must have heard him, because it suddenly started to jingle, just like it did the last time I'd visited. Mr. Haven rolled his eyes in annoyance. "It seems to be our fate," he muttered. "Whenever we're about to have a conversation . . ."

He pulled his cell phone out of his pants pocket, glanced at it, and suddenly looked as though he'd much rather be talking to the caller than to me.

"Answer it if you want to," I said nicely. As long as he didn't rush out of the apartment again right after the call . . .

Mr. Haven's lips moved as though they were saying "Excuse me," and the next minute he disappeared from the living room.

I put my Coke down and looked around. Nothing had changed; everything looked exactly the same as yesterday. Even the empty glass was still standing untouched on the newspaper on the now dried-up water stain. I wrinkled my nose, reached for the glass, and placed it a little bit farther away from me. This was hopeless! Mr. Haven would have to get used to being a bit tidier.

As I lifted the newspaper to fold it up, I saw a small, open map of Berlin underneath it. There was a felt-tip pen next to it. A few places on the map had been marked in red. The marks made the pattern that was in all the Berlin newspapers that day.

Six red marks.

Six kidnappings.

I stared in horror at the red squiggles. There's a saying that some people can't put two and two together. Which might be true, although it's not my fault that I always get four.

At least almost always.

Winter swept over the living room again. I felt as cold as if somebody had turned my heart into a giant ice cube. Oscar's kidnapping hadn't been announced until the special edition of the news yesterday evening. But the six red marks on the map in front of me had already been drawn in yesterday afternoon when I'd visited Mr. Haven. Mr. Haven had known about Oscar's kidnapping hours before the rest of the world had found out about it! And there was something else . . .

The jingle-jangle man said if I tell on him . . .

I'd just heard the jingle on Mr. Haven's cell phone again — mice running over the keyboard of a piano.

Cold and colder. Ice-cold.

As I got up from the sofa as carefully as possible, I almost thought I heard a snap, like when you break an icicle off a gutter. I crept to the door of the living room and peered into the hall. I could hear Mr. Haven talking quietly but angrily in his kitchen, and what I heard made all the hairs on my arms stand up on end.

". . . only got the two thousand euros together after you had gone public with your tragic story to try and persuade some bank or other to give you a free loan! You don't quite seem to understand what an impossible position you've put me in by doing that! I'm sorry, but the boy's life isn't worth a bean now . . ."

A heartbeat later I was outside in the stairway. Another heartbeat later it occurred to me that I hadn't pushed the newspaper back over the map. I whirled around, but it was too late. The door to Mr. Haven's apartment slammed shut with a thunderous *KAZAM!*

As if things weren't bad enough already.

Behind the door Mr. Haven called out, "Rico? Rico!"

I sprinted off.

What people in thrillers always do wrong when they're being followed is run to exactly the place that's most dangerous. Not me.

In the time it took Mr. Haven to figure out what I had found out in his living room, I didn't run downstairs to our apartment, where the two-faced kidnapper would look for me right away. Instead I scampered up a floor as fast and as quietly as I could. I always had the KKs' key in my jeans pocket so that I didn't lose it. Now I let myself into the rooftop apartment and pulled the door behind me so that it was only open a tiny crack, and listened.

Not a moment too soon. A door opened on the stairs and then Mr. Haven's voice called, "Rico?"

I heard his footsteps going quickly downstairs to the second floor. Heard him ringing our bell. Heard him knocking on our door, then banging it hard.

"Rico?"

There was silence for a few seconds. He was thinking. He was arriving at the most obvious explanation: that I must have raced out of the building, who knows where, probably to the nearest police station to tell them I'd found the kidnapper. Finally steps again, coming up the stairs. I held my breath. They stopped on the floor below me. As quietly as I could, I pressed the door shut and pressed my back against it. I waited. And thought.

Waiting was the easy part. What was I supposed to do now? I didn't want to go downstairs. Mr. Haven was probably listening for every noise in the building and would catch me on the fourth floor right away. If I shouted out a window, he'd be up here faster than anybody else. He looked like somebody who could easily break down a front door.

OK, what else could I do? In the apartment directly below me Mr. Fitz was probably mooching around, listening for any noise—and almost certainly mean enough to hand me over to Mr. Haven with an icy smile! He would ask only for my head, because he collected children's heads and played football with them in his stinky den, and the only thing missing from his collection was the head of a child proddity.

I couldn't go any farther up, either, other than out onto the roof terrace. From there I could escape over the roofs of the next-door buildings—provided I didn't fall. If that happened, all I'd be able to do was wave to Mrs. Darling as I flew past and thank her for all the whole wheat crackers, and that would be it.

SPLAT!

I could work my way around the partition onto Mr. Marrak's roof terrace. With a bit of luck his terrace door would be open; it was a hot summer's day, after all. But then? Mr. Marrak was probably at his girlfriend's, bringing her more laundry or kissing her for a change. Then I'd be stuck in his apartment instead of in here. And even if Mr. Marrak was at home, he wouldn't believe me. I knew he couldn't stand me any more than Mr. Kirk or Mr. Fitz could. Suddenly I had the terrible feeling that all kinds of people only treated me nicely because they thought they should feel sorry for me. In any case, Mr. Marrak would think I was being silly and—even worse—drag me off to say sorry to Mr. Haven.

Mr. Haven would wait until Mr. Marrak had gone and then cut me into little strips, put them in a box, and send them to Mom, while Oscar's strips were winging their way to his dad at the same time.

The simple ideas only come to you right at the end of lots of difficult thinking. My gaze wandered across the hall and landed on the telephone. That was more than just an idea—that could save me! Luckily the suspicious KKs hadn't hidden it in one of the locked rooms just in case I called one of those expensive phone numbers.

I went to the phone, picked it up, and stared at it. I don't know Mom's cell phone number by heart. That's why Mom wrote the number down twice for me. One of the pieces of paper is stuck above our own telephone in the hall-way, next to the mirror with the little fat cherubs. I put the other piece of paper in my pocket and then I lost it, of course. Since then I've meant to write the number down again a thousand times, and I've forgotten to do it a thousand times.

And look where I am now.

Then I grinned. There's one telephone number that I do know by heart. It only has three numbers. Even someone like me can learn it. Mom made me repeat it at breakfast for weeks on end: "Who do you call if you're in trouble and you can't reach me?"

I took a deep breath, dialed the emergency services, and listened hard. It took a long time for somebody to pick up.

If Mr. Haven had been after me with a knife, I thought, he would have sawed off my nose and both my ears in that time. Then, finally, as I was starting to think I'd dialed the wrong number—

"Emergency," a man's voice squawked into my ear. "How can I help?"

All at once everything was too fast for me. I hadn't thought about what I wanted to say. Now I was confused before I'd even had time to get confused.

"Hello?" I said nervously.

"Emergency services. Speak up, please!"

"My . . . my name is Frederico Doretti," I stammered. "I'm a child proddity. That's why I can only walk in a straight line and I would like to report a kidnapper. Hello?"

"Young man, listen to me—"

"Mr. 2000!" I shouted. "The ALDI kidnapper who abducted Oscar, the one without the helmet! I know where he lives! Please, you have to believe me!"

There was a quiet whistle from the telephone, as though somebody was breathing out very slowly in an effort not to lose patience. Who knows how many people called him every day, I thought, to report Mr. 2000, when they were really just playing a trick on the police? I might die because of them!

"Really?" said the man finally. "Where are you, kid?"

"Mr. 2000 lives at 93 Dieffe Street in Kreuzberg," I said very slowly and very clearly and very proudly. "On the fourth floor, in the front building on the left or the right. Mr. Haven.

I mean, he's really called East . . . no, Westhaven. Simon Westhaven!"

I took a deep breath. There was a short break on the line, as though the compass points had confused the emergency man, too. Then an angry voice said, "Listen, young man. I can see your number on my display! If you call here again interfering with operations—"

DISPLAY: A lighty-up thing that shows all kinds of stuff, like phone numbers, for example, or the price at the cash register in the supermarket or the title of the movie in the DVD player. It's a funny word and I don't really know why everybody uses it. You could just as well say "lighty-up thing."

I couldn't believe it. I hung up the phone quickly without letting the man finish. I should have known from the start no one would believe me. At least nobody could complain that I hadn't tried. But it didn't really get me any further, either.

Keep calm, Rico!

It couldn't be all that difficult to concentrate a bit and think clearly. Seeing as how I was trapped at the KKs', I might as well think about what might happen next with Oscar and Mr. Haven. Oscar was, after all, in much bigger danger than before. Mr. Haven didn't give a bean for his life. Beans come in cans, so maybe he was keeping Oscar in a can factory.

Nonsense.

Where do you hide somebody that you've kidnapped? It depends how you treat them. If you make sure they have enough to eat and drink and that there's a toilet nearby, you can keep them pretty far away from you because the victim can take care of himself. But Mr. Haven's victims were small children. They could stand in front of a packed fridge and still go thirsty and hungry and wet themselves with fear. Then he'd be in trouble. No, the longer I thought about it, the more convinced I was that Mr. Haven was keeping the kidnapped children somewhere nearby, and . . .

Near him was near me!

Good thinking, Rico!

At this point I have to admit that it took me about two hours to figure out that last part. Well, almost three, actually. In the meantime I had moved to the KKs' kitchen. Outside it was already pitch-black. The only light coming through the windows was from the moon. There were no curtains and I didn't dare put the light on. Once he realized that I hadn't gone to the police, Mr. Haven would certainly be on the look-out for me.

I drank some water from the tap and searched the kitchen for something to eat. I knew that the fridge was empty, but I looked inside again all the same. Nothing. In a cupboard I found a box of spaghetti, but the KKs' gas stove has so many knobs and buttons it scares me. You could set out to boil an egg and suddenly the whole apartment might blow up around your ears. So I opened the box of spaghetti and sucked one dry stick after another, looking out at the building behind and waiting for the ghost of Miss Friedmann to appear, looking for her ashtray.

The uncooked spaghetti felt snappy in my mouth. *Capellini*, I concluded, without any excitement. With a sad feeling in my stomach I thought about how fat Freddy had probably thrown the string of spaghetti out the window of his room or over the roof terrace railing before the KKs had gone away. It was just the kind of thing he'd do. Everything had begun with that string of spaghetti and now everything would end with a final string of spaghetti that Mr. Haven would shove into my cutoff ear.

On the third floor of the building behind, Miss Friedmann's shadowier shadow marched past one of the windows in her old apartment. I spat out a mouthful of crunchy spaghetti bits and stared, too shocked to really be afraid. I had never seen a shadowier shadow so clearly. It came from one side, let's say from the right, moved to the other side, that must be the left, vanished for a while, came back, and disappeared in the same direction it had come from in the first place, which must be . . . left?

It doesn't matter. The shadowier shadow disappeared. And something clicked inside me. At first I thought it was the lottery balls, which up until then had been strangely quiet. But this felt and sounded different. It felt and sounded as though a few pieces of a jigsaw puzzle that up until now had been waiting patiently had just fallen into place.

Now I knew everything.

Well, almost everything.

In any case, I knew what I had to do next.

ALMOST THURSDAY
in the building behind ours

Once I'd gotten through the partition I found Mr. Marrak's roof-terrace door wide open. Even so, Mr. Marrak's apartment smelled stale and of old socks. His girlfriend must have used a really useless laundry detergent. From the hall, I peeped through the slightly open bedroom door. Mr. Marrak was alone in bed. His silhouette was moving steadily up and down. He was snoring.

SILHOUETTE: Outline or shape. Whoever thought up such a mishmash of letters? Exactly! The French! I've held a grudge against the French ever since Julie said they were good kissers. They also eat frogs and snails and things, and probably right before kissing, too. Yuck!

My heart was in my mouth. It had been almost impossible to squeeze myself through the rustling bamboo canes of the partition on the roof terrace. Then I had almost broken my neck when I slid on the slippery spiral staircase down to Mr. Marrak's apartment and only just managed to hang on to the handrail. The moon was high in the sky, but considering it was shining almost two hundred and forty thousand miles away, it was nearly as dark in here as it was in the basement of 93 Dieffe Street.

The basement . . .

That was the way—and I was almost certain of it now—that Mr. Haven moved his victims into the locked building behind ours without being noticed. The basements of the two buildings were connected. Residents aren't actually allowed to go down there—there's water everywhere. Nothing makes me as frightened as water. That's why I only peeked into the basement once, with Mom, after we had just moved onto Dieffe Street. Dim light from a single, bare bulb. Damp air. A disgusting smell and dripping noises that sounded as though they came from bottomless pits. No thank you!

Mr. Haven must have unloaded the children from the trunk of his car and dragged them into the building after they had been knocked unconscious and were all tied up so that nobody noticed them, maybe in a large suitcase or a big laundry bag like Mr. Marrak's. Then past the superintendent's ground-floor apartment into the basement, through the pitch-black *splish-splash* and everything else, and finally up into the building behind ours, where he kept the children prisoner on the third floor until their ransom money had been paid. Mr. Haven stuck sticky tape over their mouths or gagged them with stinky old hankies so that they couldn't scream. And whenever he went to see them to bring them something to eat or let them go to the bathroom and stuff, the shadowier shadows crept past the windows in Miss Friedmann's apartment.

That's how far I'd got with my thinking while sucking on dry sticks of spaghetti. But then there was a gap—something was missing, and this something wouldn't stop bothering me. It had to do with forward or backward, with right or left, with before or after, but I just couldn't figure it out. At one point the lottery machine in my head had been drumming so hard that I was afraid the KKs would come back from their vacation to find me on their kitchen table with an overcooked brain. A fine mess. So I'd given up.

My eyes got used to the darkness in Mr. Marrak's apartment faster than I expected. I left my search of the bedroom for last—with Mr. Marrak in there snoring, that was the most dangerous place. Hopefully I would find what I was looking for in one of the other rooms. I felt my way all over the place at a snail's pace. Nothing—but then . . .

I didn't think there'd be anything of interest in the bathroom, but when there were no other rooms left, I thought I might as well take a look. It was kind of an excuse not to go into the bedroom yet. The tiled floor was covered in splashes of water. Mr. Marrak must have taken a shower before going to bed. At least that was something, I thought, even if he's still a pig because he doesn't air out his stinky apartment. His work clothes were scattered all over the floor in dark, messy piles. I almost cried out for joy: His big bunch of keys was hanging from the belt of his pants! Shaky with fear, I unclipped it as carefully as possible so that none of the hundreds of keys would begin to clink. A few of them didn't feel like keys at all. More like pieces of metal with all sorts of bits and pieces sticking out of them. Probably for opening safes and things like that. But it was the normal keys I needed.

Back outside, in front of the low door to the white-covered stairway on Mr. Marrak's roof terrace, I held my breath, trying out key after key. After about twenty of them, I found the right one and finally the door swung open. I was standing at the top of the stairs that led down into the building behind ours.

I was already drenched in sweat.

Yucky cold filled the stairway. I shivered. It was as though somebody had opened a tomb. The farther down the worn-out stairs I went, the more creepy it felt. The stairs, covered in white mold, creaked and groaned under my unsteady feet. Slime-oozing worms wriggled their way out of the dirty, damp walls and the moaning of long-lost souls clawed its way into my eardrums from the torture chambers under the deep basement.

Well, maybe not: That's what it was like in a horror film Mrs. Darling brought home once by mistake. I thought it was great and really wanted to watch to the end, unlike Mrs. Darling, who kept her face hidden behind one of her soft cushions the whole time and only peeked out occasionally to grab another wheat cracker. I don't know why she was so worked up.

It was really very cold and dark in the stairway because of the boarded-up windows. It was as though somebody had tied a scarf around my eyes. But I wasn't afraid. Well, all right, I was a little. The important thing was to be careful not to think about anything creepy. That was easy. In the last few hours I'd done so much thinking that my head felt like a washing machine on the spin cycle, and there was no way I could do any more. What I really had to make sure of was that I didn't take a wrong step in the dark. There was a reason why this building had been locked up after the gas explosion. Oscar had said that "in danger of collapse" meant every step under my feet and every bit of wall I leaned against could break as soon as I touched it.

On the other hand, Mr. Haven couldn't have had any problems. And he'd had to come up from the basement every time; it wasn't as far for me. I reached the fifth floor pretty quickly, and it was only a couple of floors down to the third.

More fiddling with the keys. I knew that would happen. That was the most difficult part, without a flashlight or any other lamp, but this time it was even quicker than up on the roof. Just a few tries, and suddenly I was in dead Miss Friedmann's apartment. The bunch of keys from Mr. Marrak's security business was the best!

I pressed the door shut behind me and called out Oscar's name quietly and nervously. No reply. He had to be hidden in one of the back rooms. He was probably lying in a corner full of straw and hay, gagged and out cold.

The apartment was totally empty. No furniture, no ghosts, nothing. It smelled of dust and soot, and the slight scent of those pretty purple flowers floated in the air. Violets. That had to be Miss Friedmann's perfume. It had not only survived the gas explosion and the fire in the apartment, but all the years that had gone by since then, too. The thought made me really sad for some reason.

I crept through the hall, past the bathroom, the kitchen, and the first room. Nothing and nobody inside. From the outside, a pale light fell through the dirty windowpanes. I nearly had a heart attack when I thought I saw Mr. Haven in his brightly lit kitchen in the front building across the yard. But there was no sign of the monster himself, just steam rising from a small pan on the stove. Mr. Haven surely wouldn't have left that alone if he intended to check up on Oscar. But maybe he was cooking him something to eat.

I had to get a move on.

In Mr. Fitz's, the apartment opposite Mr. Haven's, the curtains were drawn. A light was shining behind them. I wondered what the old stinker was doing. Probably counting his collection of kids' heads.

I walked along to the end of the hall to where a door led to the two rooms at the back of the apartment.

Locked.

Try the keys.

Success after lots of—well, about nine—tries.

Door open and in I go.

Now I could see my own room through the window. It was below me and a little bit to one side. It was dark, of course, but the creepy thought occurred to me that the light might suddenly go on over there and I would see Rico looking over at me, scared, from his window, because at that moment he could see my shadowier shadow.

Oh God, oh God!

If I were Mr. Haven, I would have taken the window out or boarded it up, I thought. Then I realized that everybody in the front building would have noticed. So it was better to wait for the cover of night and to play shadowier shadows. And up until now it had worked perfectly. What a sneaky man!

"Oscar?"

Still no answer.

I was getting more and more nervous. I was slowly running out of rooms. But not out of keys. I figured out the next door in a flash. The fact that it was locked made me hopeful. I pushed it open carefully. Pitch-black blackity blackness. The little moonlight that came from the connecting room wasn't enough to light the farthest corners of the space.

"Oscar?"

I stepped in blindly, five, six steps. Then two things happened at once: Miss Friedmann's violet scent turned into the smell of a Quarter Pounder with Cheese. And I banged my knee and my forehead so hard against a wall that I gave a muffled shout and swore.

"You found my airplane, didn't you?" said a quiet voice.

My knee and forehead were forgotten right away. I grinned so widely that I thought the corners of my mouth would meet over my head.

"Only by chance," I answered. "It was in the trash can."

"And after that you went to see Sophia."

"Yes, but she didn't tell me anything. She was afraid for you. I figured out everything myself, by thinking."

Well, almost everything. I could tell him about the clue Sophia didn't realize she'd given me, the one about the jingle-jangle man, later. For now it was enough being able to really impress Oscar.

"I'm glad you're here," said his voice. "Where did you get the key from?"

"Stole it from Mr. Marrak."

"Very clever. OK, now lock the door again."

"Why?"

"Because there's a contact switch built in to it. The light only goes on when the door is closed and locked, so no one outside can see it."

"I didn't know there were things like that."

"It's similar to a fridge, just the other way around."

Imagining something the other way around is always very difficult, especially when you have difficulties imagining it the right away around. "Are you trying to say," I thought out loud, "that there's no light on in a fridge when it's closed?"

Oscar gave a quiet groan.

"Are you hurt?" I asked.

"Just lock the door," came the reply.

It took a while, and a dangerous amount of jangling, until I found the key I had come in with. Oscar waited without saying another word.

When the light finally went on, I saw through scrunched-up eyes that he was crouching on an old, worn-out mattress, surrounded by a load of plastic bags and McDonald's wrappers and dozens of empty Coke cans. What a pigsty! Mr. Haven had put large cushions against the wall. They looked as though they were filled with cotton. The ceiling was covered in them, too, and a lonely energy-saving lightbulb was dangling down from the middle. I'd seen things like this in thrillers. Padded cells to stop the noise — if you shouted in here, nobody outside could hear you.

The cushions were light green. *The green room*, I thought, and for the first time since I'd set off, an ice-cold shiver ran down my spine.

Oscar himself looked spotless. Well, he'd only been locked in here since yesterday. But somehow I had pictured him in torn clothes, with a dirty face and stuff. Without his blue helmet he looked a bit helpless, and his sticky-out ears were really unbelievably big, but that was it. The only unusual thing was that he was fastened to the wall above him by a short chain and a cuff around one of his wrists. The chain was so short he couldn't lie down. He would even have to sleep sitting up.

That was the second cold shiver.

I looked around for a toilet. There had to be one somewhere, otherwise the room wouldn't have smelled of cheeseburgers, but of pee.

"It's out there in the hall, behind the front door," Oscar said as though he had read my thoughts. "It's just as sound-proof as this room."

So it was just as I had thought. Whenever Mr. Haven had taken a child to the bathroom, the shadowier shadows had crept through Miss Friedmann's apartment!

Oscar beamed at me with his green eyes and his large, unbrushed teeth—another thing Mr. Haven should have on his conscience—and all at once I felt the way an older brother must feel. My face turned bright red with pride. I had saved Oscar! Or nearly, at least.

"What kind of chain is that?"

"Quality steel, I would say," said Oscar. "Probably unalloyed, which means it has less than point eight percent manganese and point five percent silicon. If the percentage of either was higher, then—"

"Stop! How do I get it off you?"

He raised his right arm. "The key is with the rest."

"With the rest of what?"

"The rest of the keys! The ones in your hand."

"Why didn't you say so?"

Normally I would have been angry, but I swallowed it. You probably get a little crabby if you're forced to eat dozens of hamburgers and cheeseburgers and that sort of stuff. Before I could embarrass myself by stupidly asking how on earth Oscar could have put away so much food and above all so much Coke in such a short space of time without brown stuff running out of his nose, I realized that the garbage must have come from all six victims.

This thought bothered me somehow—I suddenly had that same nagging feeling the lottery balls in my head had rolled around in the wrong direction between the front and the back, the right and the left, the before and the after. But it was just as hard to figure it out as it had been the last time—even harder, in fact, because this time I had to concentrate on setting Oscar free.

I quickly found the key—it was the smallest of them all—and unlocked the handcuff. Oscar slipped it off and rubbed his wrist. When he got up from the mattress, his knees cracked and a tiny groan of pain slipped out of his mouth.

"Did you just sit around the whole time?" I asked.

"What do you mean *just*?" He looked at his sore wrist, and an angry horizontal line appeared on his forehead. "Sitting is a very complicated matter."

ALMOST THURSDAY AGAIN
the escape

Dear Mr. Meyer,

I don't want to hear any complaints about the diary getting serious at this point! The following events were dramatic, and you should be happy that they even let me write my diary in the hospital.

It's time for you to start thinking about my bonus.

Yours sincerelier,
Frederico Doretti

Walking seemed to be less complicated than sitting, or at least Oscar didn't complain. Through the window in one of the front rooms I checked that there was still a light on in Mr. Haven's apartment. There was. You could even see the child-chopper-upper himself. He was getting something to drink from the fridge and talking on his cell phone. He was probably being rude to Oscar's dad again. All the better. If Oscar and I didn't make the building collapse, we could sneak out unnoticed and tell the police. They would probably believe Oscar if he was standing there in front of them, in the flesh. Unlike me alone, who'd they'd just say was a proddity. But we had to get a move on before Mr. Haven remembered his beans.

Once we were in the boarded-up stairway, we held on to each other's hands. It was as black as coal again. As I took the first step up to the little white house on the roof, Oscar pulled me back with a start. It was strange to hear his voice without seeing him.

"Are you crazy?" he hissed. "We'll run right into him if we go that way!"

"We'll run right into him if we go down there," I answered. "He comes up through the basement, after all."

"Which basement?"

"The one he brought you up through."

Maybe it was the darkness that was making Oscar so slow to understand. Maybe, I thought, child prodigies are only really smart when it's light.

"Why should he bring me through the basement?" Oscar said.

"Because he's got no other way of getting into the building."

"*You* got here!"

Slowly he was beginning to get on my nerves. While we were blabbing on here in the dark, Mr. Haven might be drawing closer.

"I came through Mr. Marrak's roof terrace," I explained, forcing myself to be patient. "Through the little white stairway house. Don't you remember? With Mr. Marrak's keys. How is Mr. Haven supposed to get ahold of those?"

"Mr. Haven?" Oscar's voice sounded clueless. "What does this have to do with Mr. Haven?"

And that was the third shiver down my back. It was also the third time I got that feeling I had gone in the wrong direction with my thoughts somewhere—but now it was no longer a nagging feeling but a feeling that sank its teeth in me and wouldn't let go. I was a complete idiot! I was the biggest child proddity of all the child proddities in the world! My mistake had nothing to do with right or left, forward and back. It was a mistake with before and after: Mr. Haven had only been living at 93 Dieffe Street for a week! But I had seen the shadowier shadows much, much earlier—the first time had been a few months ago when the kidnappings had begun. Why and how would Mr. Haven have brought his victims here?

Suddenly a light went on in my head.

"It's not Mr. Haven—it's Mr. Marrak!" I whispered in horror. "Alarms, Safes, and Locks . . . Sales, Service, and something or other!"

"That's how I tracked him down," said Oscar. "Sophia remembered his jangling bunch of keys. And his red work uniform with the golden safe on it."

"And Sophia," I said. "How did you find her?"

"I asked around for her at all the grade schools in the Tempelhof neighborhood."

"Why her? Why not one of the other children?"

"She was the second victim. And there were photos in the newspapers. Sophia looked like she would talk if she knew anything."

"The bunch of keys and the red uniform," I repeated quietly. "Mr. Marrak. Oh God, oh God! Sophia should have told the police!"

"She was afraid!"

"She's still afraid. But then *you* should have told the police."

Oscar was quiet. I could picture him talking to Sophia. How Sophia told him things you would only tell another kid. How she gave Oscar her little red airplane, happy that she had somebody to talk to. How Oscar, just as happy, pinned on the airplane, a little boy with a blue helmet on his head who normally didn't have any friends because he was too brainy.

"I promised her I wouldn't tell," Oscar murmured. "My mom always said you shouldn't break promises."

I swallowed. Something was pressing against my shoulders and my heart as though the darkness was crushing us. "And then?" I whispered.

"Then I copied down the contact details for all the security companies in Berlin from the phone book," Oscar continued. "Every afternoon after school I went to look for them, one by one. It took weeks. I eventually found Mr. Marrak by chance. The phone book only has his cell phone number, not his address. He dropped in at another security company that I happened to be watching. Maybe he was visiting a friend. I was standing on the other side of the street and saw him getting out of his car and knew I had him. At least almost. He didn't stay long. But long enough for me to hail a taxi and follow him."

"Hey, I took a taxi, too!"

"But you didn't get thrown out halfway, did you? The stupid driver turned to me at a red light and wanted to know if I could pay. I didn't have enough money with me and he refused to go any farther. I could see Mr. Marrak turning off onto Grimm Street, so I followed him on foot. His car was parked on Dieffe Street, but I didn't know which apartment building he'd disappeared into. I waited. About two hours later he left number 93. There were two possibilities. Either he had just visited a customer . . ."

". . . or he lived there," I said. "Right? And you crept around Dieffe Street to find out. And that's when you met me."

I couldn't see Oscar, but I could tell that he was nodding. I also had a bitter taste in my mouth.

"You used me to get into the building! To look for Mr. Marrak! To find out if he lived here!"

No answer again. I didn't say anything else, either. Silence spread like a jet black puddle. We should have been getting out of there. Instead we were standing in a stairway that was in danger of collapse, unable to see our own hands in front of our faces and not knowing what to say to each other—me because of disappointment, and Oscar because he didn't know how to say sorry.

"In the beginning," he said finally, and was quiet again for a second. "In the beginning I didn't care about you. I really just wanted to get into the building. But up on the roof terrace—"

"— where you finally found what you wanted—"

"—I was sorry that I'd used you. I like you, Rico! You were never mean to me, and you risked your life to find me. You're my only friend." His last words were a whisper. "You still are."

I grumbled a little bit. I didn't have another friend besides Oscar. It's strange how people are just as clueless about what to do with somebody who's not that bright as they are with somebody who's really intelligent. I thought of the afternoon on the roof terrace and how Oscar had held my hand. That had been really nice, and not a lie at all. I had felt it.

"How did you get yourself kidnapped?" I said at last.

I heard him breathe out with relief. "That was simple. I planned it for Tuesday morning, but then I changed my mind because I'd promised to visit you."

"Without your helmet?" I said, hardly able to believe it.

"I'm not as afraid when you're with me," Oscar murmured quietly, and continued speaking quickly as though it was embarrassing. "I took the subway to your station and walked toward Dieffe Street. But on Grimm Street, Mr. Marrak was coming in my direction and got into his car."

I felt all dizzy. I had seen Mr. Marrak going out of the building from the living room window! He must have bumped into Oscar, or Oscar into him, not a minute later.

"I couldn't miss the opportunity!" Oscar said. "So I asked him if he could take me with him—told him my dad hadn't come home the night before and I wanted to go and look for him and, um, you know . . . the kind of things you make up on the spot."

Or if it's really happened to you before, I thought.

"Anyway, he took me with him. We only went past three traffic lights. By then I had made sure to give him Dad's phone number, and Mr. Marrak sprayed something in my face. I didn't wake up until the afternoon, when he pulled me out of the laundry bag in his apartment. I was handcuffed and tied up and a bit fuzzy in the head, but I had—"

"You were in his laundry bag?"

"I think so. That's what it looked like."

I didn't know what upset me more: that Mr. Marrak, after drugging Oscar in the morning and somehow tying him up without being noticed, had gone about his work perfectly calmly until the afternoon. Or that I had met him on the stairs and talked to him while Oscar had been bundled up in a bag at our feet. That part, I decided, I would only tell Oscar much later. I was really shocked by that—not to mention the fact that Mr. Marrak probably didn't have a girlfriend who did his laundry or anything like that.

"But in the meantime I had almost managed to somehow get one arm free," Oscar was saying. "And when Mr. Marrak dragged me over to the little white house on his roof terrace,

I recognized it, tore the red airplane off my shirt without him noticing, and threw it over the railing."

"But why? Mr. Marrak would have freed you once your dad had paid the ransom, if not before. Then you could have been a witness against him and everybody would have had to believe you."

For a while all I could hear was Oscar breathing. "I wasn't sure," he finally said quietly, "whether my dad would . . . whether he would get the money together quickly enough. Stuff like that."

The last sentence sounded very sad, as though Oscar wasn't sure if his dad would have paid the ransom money for him at all.

"And if that was the case," he said, still quietly, "you were my only hope. There was only a tiny little chance, but it was obviously big enough."

There was another silence.

"A long story," a voice rang out above us. "But thank you for the revealing explanation!"

A beam of light flashed on and dazzled us.

Oscar and I screamed at the same time. We ran at the same time, too—down the stairs. Mr. Marrak, who had been listening from a few steps farther up, thundered after us, which was lucky in a funny way, because his flashlight lit up the way not only for him, but for us, too. We jumped and crashed our way through the building, and I decided whoever had said it was in danger of collapse was completely stupid—it was clearly bombproof.

At the bottom of the stairs, we stood in front of the door that led out to the backyard. It was locked. I pressed the bunch of keys into Oscar's hand. He was cleverer than I was.

"You do it!" I hissed. "I'll talk to him!"

Mr. Marrak crashed down behind us like somebody who'd taken a running jump into a swimming pool and found it was empty. His flashlight fell to the ground with a bang and rolled away. Dust flew up into the air. In the beam of light from the floor I could see Oscar standing next to me without moving, as though now was the moment he had chosen to try out how it felt to be a tree or a traffic light or something. I think it's called being frozen with fear. Behind him three shadows were stuck to the wall: two small ones and one giant one.

"End of the line!" said Mr. Marrak.

If you could weigh anger, then his weighed at least a ton or even more. A lot, in any case. I had no idea how I was going to stop him, to give us some time and to unfreeze Oscar. But I would have to think of something. I could feel the lottery machine slowly starting up. If I waited five more seconds, it would be too late. So I threw him the first best question I could think of, like throwing a bone at a guard dog, though I would rather have asked it really casually over a cup of hot chocolate or something. Preferably while there were bars between us, with him in a maximum-security prison.

"Why did you phone Oscar's dad after the kidnapping instead of writing him a letter like you usually do?"

Mr. Marrak glared at me nastily, but his answer shot out as though from a gun. "To hurry things up," he growled. "So that I could get rid of this irritating super-smarty-pants as fast as possible!"

Oscar didn't even bat an eyelid in his deep freeze as the brawny face of his kidnapper pushed right in front of his.

"You are the weirdest and most irritating child I have ever met!" Mr. Marrak snorted at him. "Do you know how they would have treated you in the Middle Ages? Like a freak! Like a punishment from God! Brats like you would have been burned at the stake four hundred years ago!"

"The Middle Ages," Oscar said scornfully, "ended more than *five* hundred years ago. The Renaissance began after that, you ignoramus!"

I had never heard of the Renaissance, but it must have been terrible, because Mr. Marrak winced. For a moment I was afraid he would hit Oscar. Instead he put on the sweetest face of all time. In crime thrillers that's always a sign that the criminal's gone loopy and has bats in the belfry. Mr. Marrak, and I was one hundred percent certain of this, didn't even have a belfry.

"I actually like children!" he said in a sugary-sweet voice. "I really like them, in fact. But their parents should keep a closer eye on them. That's all I ever wanted! It's a bad world out there. I didn't care about the money. Yes, yes, it's true,

I like children. Even educationally challenged ones!"

Now he spun around with a jerk and turned to me. Over his shoulder I was glad to see that Oscar had finally snapped out of it. He began to fiddle with the lock carefully and without making a sound.

"But I like my freedom, too!" Mr. Marrak breathed right into my face. His grin was as lopsided as if somebody had sliced a clown's mask in two, right down the middle. "You shouldn't have stuck your nosy nose into my business, Rico Doretti! Now I'm afraid I'll have to cut it off."

He took a step toward me.

I wrinkled my brow.

That wasn't right.

"You're doing it in the wrong order," I said.

Mr. Marrak paused, puzzled. "Which order?"

"The cutting-off part. The ears come first." I began to list everything, mightily proud that I'd remembered all Felix had told me.

"Kidnappers always cut the ears off first. Both of them. Then one hand, and then—"

"You stupid little—"

"Please don't interrupt me!"

Honestly, when you finally remember something, someone like that comes along! I was so angry I just kept going, shouting:

"And then the arm that belongs to it! The other one has to stay on so that you can still write begging letters! But I'll tell you right now, the most my mom can do is crack open the piggy bank for you! And, well . . . that's it!"

It felt really good to shout at Mr. Marrak, even though I must admit that what I had to say wasn't particularly sensible. If he wasn't going to get any money out of Mom, he could saw off both my arms before moving on to the legs. Luckily for me, however, he had no time to think of that himself.

Behind him, there was a *click*.

The door flew open. Pale, milky moonlight poured into the stairway. I shot past Mr. Marrak like a bolt of lightning.

If Oscar hadn't been so small, I might not have tripped over him. I have no idea why he didn't sprint off at the same time. He could even have had a head start, but he seemed to be waiting for me. I bowled right into him in the middle of the doorway.

Both of us fell. I crashed into the backyard next to Oscar and slid over the rough, hard ground on one elbow. I could feel it starting to bleed. Then something heavy hit me in the stomach and there was a shout as Mr. Marrak tripped over me and fell to the ground like a tree that had been chopped down. Next to me Oscar got to his feet and stretched out a hand. I grabbed it and got up with a groan.

"Quick! Let's go!" I coughed.

We took off again, Oscar in front of me, but I was quicker than Oscar and overtook him to reach the large door to our building first.

The large, sticking door!

I pressed both hands down on the handle and pulled with all my strength on the part that was supposed to open, but it barely moved—two or three inches at most! The crack that opened up was too small even for Oscar to slip through.

I spun around, the hard door at my back. Oscar pressed himself against me, his arms around my waist. In the moonlight I could see that Mr. Marrak had got back on his feet. He stared at us with wild eyes, then charged like a raving-mad bull.

"Police!" cried a voice above us. My head shot up. Up above, on the fourth floor, Mr. Haven was standing in the window, a pistol in his outstretched right hand. "Don't move or I'll have to shoot!"

But Mr. Marrak had already caught up to us. He reared above Oscar and me like a mountain. I covered Oscar's head with my arms to protect him, then stared right into Mr. Marrak's eyes. Unfortunately Mom and Oscar are a lot better at the staring trick than I am. It didn't work at all.

The last thing I heard was a loud roar. The last thing I saw were two things coming down from the sky, one above me and one above Mr. Marrak. What came down on me was Mr. Marrak's fist. It hit me right on the forehead and, as I slowly fell over and everything went black, Mr. Marrak made a strange face, grabbed his bleeding forehead, and fell over, too.

*　*　*

Millions of years later I came to. I was being carried through the entrance hall to our apartment building. I looked up and saw Mr. Haven's face. I was in his arms. Somebody was holding the front door open, probably the superintendent, Mr. Mommsen. Somebody was crying, probably Mrs. Darling. Somebody was babbling on in excitement about something, probably Oscar. Flashing red and blue lights lit up the street in front of 93 Dieffe Street, but I was still looking up at Mr. Haven. It was like in a dream: I could hear my own voice murmuring, and Mr. Haven held me close to his chest and listened to every word.

"One day my dad went out in a boat with friends, off the coast of Naples. It was a stormy autumn day. The waves were high and black and foamy. My dad threw out a fishing line. A very large fish took a bite; a huge struggle broke out. The fish won. It pulled Dad overboard. My dad drowned in the deep blue sea."

THURSDAY
bright and sunny

Mom has just visited me in the hospital. Nobody else has been allowed in yet: not Mr. Haven, not Mrs. Darling, not Bert. Not Mr. Kirk or Mr. Mommsen, either, even though it's nice that both of them have asked about me. They won't even let Oscar in; I won't see him until tomorrow. And all because of a little bump on the head!

"The press is waiting down there." Mom was standing at the window of my private room, looking out. "They're lining up as far back as the canal."

"Will I be famous now?"

She sighed. "You will. There's no way around it. You and Oscar. But only for a few days. We live in a fast world that forgets fast."

When she first came in and took me carefully in her arms without saying a word, I started to cry right away. She was wearing black clothes that made her look as dark as midnight, and her face looked very worried. I thought it was all my fault. But that wasn't true. Uncle Christian had died the day before.

I knew that Mom hadn't gotten along well with him, but he was her brother all the same.

Mom came up to Berlin because of me, though she had to go back down to the bottom and left again after a while, because of the funeral and everything. I felt really sorry for her, but I was happy that Uncle Christian would lie in his coffin without me after all. I was sure it would be more comfortable for him that way, too.

"Do you know what the crazy thing is?" Mom said, and came over from the window to sit on the edge of my bed. "The crazy thing is that Christian bequeathed everything to me. He didn't have anybody else. It's sad somehow, don't you think?"

"What does *bequeath* mean?"

"He left everything to us. The money, the car, everything."

"Are we rich now?"

"Depends on how you look at it. He had a house, too."

"Do we have to move now?" I called out in fear.

"We don't have to." Mom stroked my bandaged arm. She looked deep into my eyes. "But we will."

That was the last straw! It's difficult to think when you've got a concussion. But something inside me thought all by itself: that I would lose Oscar as a friend if I had to move to the bottom and left on the map, and Mrs. Darling and the whole wheat crackers, too. That I would have to go to another school before Mr. Meyer had read my summer vacation diary. That it would never work out with Mr. Haven and Mom and that there was definitely no bingo club at the bottom and left.

How could Mom have made such a decision without talking to me about it? I looked at her, horrified, and wondered what there was to grin about.

"You know, I hear," she said very slowly, "that in a certain building on Dieffe Street there'll be an empty apartment available very soon. Up on the fifth floor. With a roof terrace. The view over Berlin is supposed to be phenomenal."

It took me a little time, and then I realized what she meant.

"We can live above Mr. Haven!" I burst out.

"Yes, Rico. Directly above a policeman."

It was still really embarrassing to me that I had got it so wrong about Mr. Haven. But how could I have known that he was not only a police detective, but also in charge of the kidnapping investigation? That's why he'd been able to put six red dots on the map before the public was told about Oscar's kidnapping. That's why he'd been talking to Oscar's stupid dad and had told him off on the cell phone. And that's why the man on the emergency number had thought I was putting him on. I had tried to tell him that the kidnapper was the police detective in charge of the investigation. Really, you wouldn't even be able to think that up with a normal brain! Well, maybe Miss Marple would have figured it out; she's a lot smarter than I am. But my butt is nowhere near as big as hers, and from now on I can ask Mr. Haven for help if anybody else gets kidnapped.

"Do you still think he's the hottest thing you've ever met in your entire life?" I asked Mom carefully.

Maybe I should have dropped it, because suddenly there it was again, the mixture of tiredness and sadness on her face that had been there in the thinking chair after Mr. Haven's visit on Monday. Only this time there was a very small smile, too. And even though Mom did not reply, and only kissed the bandage on my forehead when she said good-bye, I felt a little bit of hope come back.

Well, that's it. Vacation time for my vacation diary. I have to take a break so that the lottery machine can sort itself out. I wrote all of the last part by hand, in the notebook I asked Mom to bring. Next week, when I'm let out of the hospital, Mr. Meyer says I have to copy it all over to the computer, because of my orthography.

> ORTHOGRAPHY: Means spelling in complicated speak. It's no wonder I find it difficult, because it's got the word GRAPH in it, so it's like math, which I've already told you isn't my strong point.

I have to get a move on, because it's nearly dinnertime and if the nurse finds out that I've spent the whole afternoon writing away secretly, there'll be trouble. She's great and very pretty, too. So I'll put the notebook away. I've actually told everything there is to tell.

Except for one thing.

Apparently Mr. Fitz kept a boulder in his stinky apartment, which is what hit Mr. Marrak right on the forehead the night he was chasing us, but the biggest question is, why were there hundreds of other stones lying around it, large and small? That's what the police found when they questioned him. But Mr. Fitz didn't want to tell anybody why, not even Mr. Haven, even though he's a neighbor, and not the people from the newspapers and the television, even though Mr. Fitz is a hero now, like Oscar and me. Mr. Fitz of all people! He grumbled that it wasn't against the law to keep stones in his apartment, and he's probably right. I'm just glad it wasn't a kid's head he chucked down into the yard that night. All the same, I think Mr. Fitz has a secret. No normal person collects stones and throws the biggest one out the window in the middle of the night, and Mr. Fitz said it wasn't to hit Mr. Marrak or us two boys screaming our heads off and disturbing his peace and quiet, but for other reasons!

Oh God!

Maybe I should tell Oscar about it tomorrow.

Yes, I'll definitely tell Oscar about it tomorrow.